PUFFIN BOOKS

FIFTH YEAR FRIEN

CW00924836

Rebecca Mason intends to devote the fifth year at Trebizon School to tennis – she must get back on top form – and stay there! For she has been spotted by the agent Herman Lasky, who is considering offering her a professional contract, but she has to put everything into it if she is to succeed. Robbie Anderson is pleased that her future, unlike his, seems clear.

Life becomes complicated when Rebecca realizes that she may have to forgo not only a trip to Paris, but hopes of getting the good GCSE grades that ensure her a place in the sixth form. But why should she care? Rebecca, as Robbie's sister Tish realizes, is refusing to face up to the difficult choice ahead: for she wants to stay at Trebizon more than anything. Until, with a sudden aching sense of loss, she realizes the friendships she'd be leaving behind . . .

Added to all this is the worrying mystery of little Naomi Cook, who is accused of stealing things from the junior boarding house, including Holly Thomas's Walkman and Jay Larcombe's new blazer. Rebecca alone believes in Naomi, but it is her friend Cliff Haynes who unexpectedly gives her the key to the mystery.

The twelfth story about Rebecca and her friends has all the drama and excitement we have come to love in this universally popular Trebizon series.

Anne Digby was born in Kingston upon Thames, Surrey, but lived in the West Country for many years. As well as the Trebizon books, she is the author of the popular *Me, Jill Robinson* series.

ANNE DIGBY

FIFTH YEAR
FRIENDSHIPS AT
TREBIZON

PUFFIN BOOKS

For Anna with love
(and thanks)

PUFFIN BOOKS

Published by the Penguin Group
27 Wrights Lane, London w8 5 tz, England
Viking Penguin Inc., 40 West 23rd Street, New York, New York 10010, USA
Penguin Books Australia Ltd, Ringwood, Victoria, Australia
Penguin Books Canada Ltd, 2801 John Street, Markham, Ontario, Canada l 3 r 1 b 4
Penguin Books (NZ) Ltd, 182–190 Wairau Road, Auckland 10, New Zealand

Penguin Books Ltd, Registered Offices: Harmondsworth, Middlesex, England

First published 1990
10 9 8 7 6 5 4 3 2 1

Copyright © Anne Digby, 1990
All rights reserved

Filmset in 10/12pt Linotron Ehrhardt by
Rowland Phototypesetting Ltd, Bury St Edmunds, Suffolk
Printed and bound in Great Britain by
Cox and Wyman Ltd, Reading, Berks

CONTENTS

ONE

FEELING FAMOUS

'Please can you have my *what*?' asked Rebecca Mason over the noise of the speeding coach. She stopped sucking the end of her biro and glanced up. She was in the middle of composing a letter to her French pen-friend. 'My *scarf*? What's the matter, Naomi? Cold?'

'Your *autograph*,' repeated the First Year girl, slightly embarrassed now but refusing to be put off. A piece of paper appeared under Rebecca's nose. 'Please can you write something for me? I saw you on TV on Boxing Day. You were really good! It was like watching Wimbledon. You're famous now.'

'Oh, the school film!' laughed Rebecca, startled. No one had ever asked her for an autograph before; well, not on this basis. Was this how it felt, feeling famous? (Was this how it might be one day, people asking for your autograph?)

'I wish I were, Naomi!' she said. 'You should have seen how horribly I played in the Midland Indoor last week.'

I was pathetic, she thought. And to think I won it last year! I got knocked out in the quarter finals. Call that famous?

All the same, her scalp tingled quite pleasurably.

'You'll soon be famous now your arm's better, now you've been on TV and people see how brilliant you really are,' said the younger girl confidently. 'I could tell you were good even with your other arm slung up in that sling. Last term. When Miss Willis made you play in those foursomes. That must have been difficult.'

'I'll say,' agreed Rebecca. 'It was nice of you juniors to ball-girl for me sometimes.'

'Miss Willis made us do it.'

Rebecca laughed again. 'Well, that's honest!' She took the piece of paper from Naomi. She rested it on the pad on her knee and sucked the biro again, planning what to write. She thought of a little poem:

HONESTLY SPEAKING

I said 'thanks', expecting you
To say: 'Oh, nothing to it.'
I nearly died when you replied:
'Miss Willis made us do it.'

Best wishes to Naomi

Rebecca Mason [V Alpha]

Naomi took it back eagerly and read it. It was the first time Rebecca had seen her smile! 'That's really good. I'll cut it out and paste it in my autograph book.'

Rebecca's eyes strayed back to her writing pad.

'OK, then? Got to get on with this letter now.'

They were on the long-distance coach, returning to their boarding school, Trebizon, for the spring term. Rebecca's parents were in Saudi Arabia as usual, and she'd spent the

Christmas holidays in Gloucestershire with her grandmother. Nobody else from Trebizon used this coach as a
rule. Most of the girls returned to school via the train from
London, or else were brought by car. Some of the girls in the
Upper Sixth drove back themselves in their own cars.

Earlier, Rebecca had grabbed a seat to herself and
sprawled in luxury, text books and writing paper spread
around her, as well as some GCSE history coursework that
she hoped to complete on the journey. It was supposed to be
handed in to Miss Maggs tomorrow morning, the first day of
term. Maggy would kill them if it weren't finished! But first
she was going to revise some French vocabulary and then try
to write a brilliant letter to Emmanuelle, her French pen-
friend. Trebizon was twinned with a school in Paris. There
was going to be a French exchange this year!

Sometime in the Easter holidays, the dates weren't quite
fixed yet, a group of them from Trebizon's Fifth would be
going to Paris. Rebecca would be staying with Emmanuelle,
who looked very nice in her photo and sounded even nicer in
her letters. Paris in the springtime. Everybody said it would
be beautiful. The river . . . the chestnut trees out in blossom
. . . and delicious things to eat and drink at pavement cafés.
And she'd have to speak French all the time – that was the
rule. Just as well, with her GCSE orals in May! She must
get an A for French. It would be pathetic if she couldn't get
an A for French, when she was supposed to be good at
languages. It was fun learning languages. Perhaps she'd
learn some more in the Sixth!

In the summer, when her parents were home on leave
and they were able to use their London house again,
Emmanuelle would come and stay with *her*. It'd be like
having a sister for a while. She'd show her Harrods and
Buckingham Palace and Oxford Street and all the other

things she said she wanted to see. And they'd try to get into the House of Commons and watch all the Members of Parliament shouting at each other! Why *did* they shout so much? They'd get into trouble at Trebizon if they behaved like that!

Some of these thoughts Rebecca translated into fairly fluent French in her letter to Emmanuelle and was deeply engrossed when the coach pulled in somewhere to pick up more passengers. She glanced dreamily out of the window, unsure where they were, even. Somewhere off the motor-way; somewhere around Bristol. Amongst the people waiting in parked cars, she recognized a familiar face pressed to the rear window of a rusted van, the expression on the face uncharacteristically sullen. She certainly remembered the new girl's face from last term as being rather withdrawn, but not sullen. Nevertheless –

'Yes, it's Naomi Cook all right,' she decided when a diminutive girl in Trebizon blue cape, with fairish hair and pale freckled face, came into her line of vision. She was walking behind a blue-faced couple, the hoods of their shabby anoraks up against the biting January wind, who humped between them a newish-looking school trunk. The trio disappeared round the back of the coach with the rest of the throng to meet the coach driver, who was now super-vising the loading on of luggage.

Naomi was almost the last person to board the coach – she seemed to forget something and had to run back to the van – but when she did, Rebecca stood up to greet her:

'Hello! Good! We can share the taxi at the other end!'

'Rebecca!'

They both knelt on Rebecca's seat, noses pressed to the window, to wave to Naomi's parents.

Mr and Mrs Cook stood in front of their van, chilly-looking, blank-faced, staring uncomprehendingly. The coach was already pulling away. Slowly it dawned on them that there was another Trebizon girl on the coach with Naomi, an older girl, and they waved back in relief.

'I didn't think there'd be anyone else from school!' said Naomi with obvious pleasure, as she settled down in the seat across the gangway from Rebecca's. 'There wasn't last time.'

'I came down by train from London,' Rebecca explained. 'That's where I go when my parents are home on leave. I use this coach the rest of the time.'

She glanced at the girl, remembering the one time they'd spoken last term. It was after one of those tennis sessions, when Naomi had been a ball-girl. She knew that the new First Year was very clever and had won the top scholarship to Trebizon. But she'd looked homesick to Rebecca.

'D'you like it here?' she'd asked.

'It's all right, except everybody seems to have pots of money. Or at least their parents do.'

'Mine don't. Lots don't, you'd be surprised. My dad's company has to pay all my school fees.'

'I just wonder sometimes if I'm going to fit in,' Naomi had said in a rush.

'That's just how *I* felt at first. It doesn't last.'

Or at least, it hadn't lasted for Rebecca. But seeing Naomi around at the end of last term, the sweet, slightly withdrawn expression had still been there. As though she were still ill at ease, being at Trebizon.

However, studying the girl's face now, on the coach, Rebecca decided that the sullen expression earlier must have been a figment of her imagination: she was definitely looking more peaceful.

'I shan't be coming on this coach any more!' she blurted out.

'You won't?'

'Mum's managed to get an exchange!'

'How do you mean?'

'A council house exchange. They're moving next week! Near Trebizon.'

'Oh, you mean you won't be boarding any more? You'll be a day-girl?'

'Oh, no! I'll still be boarding. It's too far to walk. And Dad's van's about to pack up any minute. Besides, they've bought the night-clothes and the trunk and that now and everything else is, well, free. It's just that . . . well, it'll be better, won't it?'

Rebecca wasn't too sure about that. Would it really help someone to settle down, having their family so close? Did she think she'd see a lot of them now? Juniors had to stay strictly within bounds! They weren't allowed downtown. She certainly wouldn't be allowed to pop home when she felt like it; she'd have to stick to the rules like all the other young boarders in Juniper House. It didn't really solve the problem of whether Naomi was going to like being at Trebizon or not.

But of course she said none of this.

She returned to writing her letter until, a few minutes later, back on the motorway again, Naomi leaned across and asked for that autograph.

And Rebecca had her taste of feeling famous.

TWO

ROBBIE REMEMBERS

Rebecca craned forward in the taxi as it scrunched across the gravel forecourt of Court House. She could see her friends! Their faces were pressed against the window of the ground-floor common room at the front of the building as they waved and gesticulated. They were all in there to watch TV; Rebecca could see the screen's flickering colours through the window. They must have heard the taxi arrive!

There were Tish Anderson and Sue Murdoch, her two closest friends. And Margot Lawrence, Mara Leonodis and Sally Elphinstone, otherwise known as Elf. As they all spilled out of the front door, she wound down the window of the taxi, letting in a blast of wintry air.

'Hi!' she shrieked.

'Rebecca, hurry!'

'We're running the film!'

'Tish brought the video!'

As the taxi juddered to a halt, Naomi Cook, who'd sat alongside her in silence during the brief journey from the bus station, tugged urgently at Rebecca's cape.

'Please –'

'What's the matter?'

'You know I said about being ball-girl? I said Miss Willis made us do it. Well, she *did* make us do it, but –'

'Yes?'

'I don't want you to think I didn't want to! I liked it. I know your arm's O K now but I'd still like to come and be ball-girl sometimes, whenever you want in fact.'

'Thanks, Naomi. Lovely! I'll hold you to that!' replied Rebecca with a quick smile. She was already getting out of the taxi, her friends swarming towards her. 'Elf, you've had your hair cut! It suits you!' she shouted.

The cab driver unloaded her luggage from the boot and she paid him off. 'Can you take the other passenger on to Juniper, please?' she asked him. 'Tell her I've paid.'

All juniors spent their first two years at Trebizon in Juniper House, a huge red brick building at the back of main school. The rules were strict in there; they didn't have the same freedom as the middle school pupils, who lived in smaller boarding houses around the grounds, like Court.

And then she was being swept along by her friends, all helping with the luggage, towards the front door.

'We'll leave it in the porch!'

'We can take it up later!'

'Come on, Rebecca, you're missing the video.'

A scrunching noise behind reminded Rebecca that the taxi was leaving and, as an afterthought, she turned to wave. But Naomi had already shrunk back into her seat, her face a pale triangle of light in the vehicle's dark interior.

'Good Christmas, Tish?' Rebecca asked, as they followed the others indoors.

She'd been curious that neither Tish nor her brother Robbie had phoned her these holidays. Maybe she should have phoned them. Robbie Anderson was in his last year at Garth College, a school near Trebizon.

'Awful,' grinned Tish. 'Robbie was depressed. Dad was in a foul temper. They rowed all the time. Happy Christmas!'

'Oh.'

'He's written to you. Robbie. I've got the letter in my trunk. I'll give you it later.' *A letter? Good!* thought Rebecca. 'And at least he remembered to tape the film for you. He promised, didn't he.'

'Robbie remembered!' laughed Rebecca. 'Good. Now I've got my own copy. Gran taped it too but she's locked it away in a cupboard for Mum and Dad when they come home. But how about you?'

'Robbie had a copy made.'

'Shut up, you two!' said Margot. "Come in and shut the door. This is my big moment coming up!'

Rebecca perched on the arm of the sofa and watched the black-skinned, white swimsuited Margot catch a gigantic wave on her surfboard in the shining turquoise sea. It was a glorious scene from last summer and a definite contrast to the grey winter skies outside.

They had great fun with the video: running backwards and forwards, re-running their favourite bits, picking up fresh things to comment on.

'Surely I don't look like that when I run?' exclaimed Tish.

'I look so *fat*,' wailed Elf. 'I'm going on a diet this term.'

'What again?' they all chorused.

But the six of them agreed that the documentary about life at Trebizon, made by a small film company the previous summer, had turned out brilliantly (which had not been the intention of the film company in the first place!).

And the match between Rebecca and Joss Vining,

showing Rebecca winning the final of the County Closed, made a stunning climax.

Rebecca stared at the screen, mesmerized by the way she'd played last summer! Those were probably the four best games of tennis she'd ever played in her life, captured on film for ever. The tape would be an inspiration to her.

She wouldn't rest, she told herself, until she always played like that. She must get back on top form – and stay there!

The very same day, somewhere in London, two men were watching the very same sequence.

'Interesting. How d'you pick this up, Wayne?'

'Fluke! I programmed the video to get something else – you know, Tennis Highlights of the Year, on Boxing Day. The schedule was running a few minutes late, so the tape picked up the end of this programme about life at a girls' boarding school.'

'She's still at school then?'

'Yes. But there's star quality lurking there, I'd say.'

'Find out about her, Wayne. What's her name? Is she on the computer?'

'Rebecca Mason. She played at Eastbourne last summer. Brenda was at Eastbourne, she'll know more about her.'

'OK, that's a start. Run it through again, Wayne. Let's take another look.'

'Well, I've got your tennis schedule for the term, Rebecca,' said Mrs Ericson after tea, 'and plenty of it, too.'

The county tennis coach had lost no time in driving over to Trebizon. Her most promising junior was back in the West Country! The meeting took place in Miss Willis's office, in Trebizon's sports centre. Miss Willis was out but

Miss Greta Darling, Rebecca's coach at school, took her place.

Mrs Ericson hadn't come to congratulate Rebecca for her starring 'performance' in the Trebizon film, which she neither knew nor cared about, but to upbraid her gently about the Midland 16-and-under Indoor tournament.

'I know it was your first bash since recovering from your injury, Rebecca,' she said, 'but you won it last year, so this year you should have been able to win it with the proverbial hand tied behind the back. All the older girls have moved up!'

'I know,' sighed Rebecca. 'I never really got going. If only I'd had some tough matches in the opening rounds, to *get* me going. I know I could have got my form back. But the first round was a walkover. The girl didn't show up. The second round showed up but she needn't have bothered! It was 6–0, 6–0. She'd just turned fourteen on New Year's Eve. What bad luck!' Rebecca added charitably.

They laughed.

Age classification rules in junior tennis were simple and clear-cut. Whatever your age on 1 January, that became your official age for the rest of the calendar year. So if Rebecca's second-round opponent had been born a few hours later, on New Year's Day, she'd have been playing in 14-and-under tournaments for another whole year, instead of having to play the likes of Rebecca in the 16–Us.

'But you're in a splendid position yourself, Rebecca,' Miss Darling pointed out. 'Another full year as a 16–U!'

Rebecca's birthday wasn't until July.

'Even better than you think,' added Mrs Ericson. 'D'you realize just how many girls above you on the computer had their birthdays in the autumn? A whole army of them has had to move up to 18–U!'

'Who's still left?' asked Rebecca eagerly.

'Well, Rita Sullivan and Rachel Cathcart.'

'I've beaten Rita! Remember – at Bristol last year!' said Rebecca excitedly.

She'd never played Rachel Cathcart.

'Well, if you beat them *both* at Bristol this year and then one or two others in the Prudential at Easter, you could find yourself the Number One 16–U in the country!'

Rebecca went very quiet, as this amazing thought gradually sank in. Her two coaches were rustling application forms now, talking above her head about useful tournaments, county tennis fixtures, coaching sessions at the indoor school at Exonford. Then Bristol at half-term. Rebecca didn't take in all the details but got the general gist.

'Well, you *are* going to have a heavy programme,' smiled Mrs Ericson, rising to her feet. 'Here! It's all typed out. I'll see you at Exonford on Sunday, then? Did you get your Results Sheet off by 3 January? Don't be disappointed when your new ranking comes through. You've lost three months' points, being out of competitions. We'll have you bouncing back again soon. The next lot of rankings will be a different story!'

'Honestly?'

Rebecca left the sports centre in an excited daze. She hurried along the lamplit footpaths that led across the school grounds, back to the boarding house. The wind was cold and she wrapped her school scarf round her head to stop her ears from tingling. Why did it have to get dark so early? She'd have liked to have fetched one of her tennis rackets and gone and thumped a ball relentlessly against the wall of Norris House. All night if necessary.

As soon as she got back, she pinned the typewritten tennis schedule on the notice-board in her cubicle. Then she glanced over to her work-table, guiltily. Spread out there, waiting to be done, was the rest of her history coursework. She hadn't managed to finish it on the coach, after all. She'd been about to tackle it after tea and had been summoned over to the sports centre instead.

Beside the school work lay a thick envelope. The letter from Robbie! She hadn't even had a chance to open it yet.

But the history had to be handed in to Maggy first lesson, didn't it? Not too much to do on it now. She'd promised herself to try and get all A or B grades in her GCSEs and she only had a term or so to do it in now. Mocks were in March! They were going to be in January, but the school had decided to postpone them. Even so, less than eight weeks to go! Nothing, not even tennis, must be allowed to spoil her chances.

She'd save Robbie's letter. She'd read it in bed.

She'd think about tennis tomorrow.

It was lovely and quiet. The others were all out. No excuses, then. Nothing to distract her.

Right now she was going to get her history done.

THREE

SOMETHING PLEASANT ... AND SOMETHING AMAZING

Robbie's letter was very long. Enclosed with it was his rejection letter from Oxford! It was a standard printed letter and they'd even forgotten to write his name in at the top, so it just began 'Dear—'.

'We very much regret that you have not been successful in your application to this college,' it said and ended: 'In order not to build up false hopes, we must inform you that your application is no longer being actively considered by any other college.' How brutal it sounded! How final! After all his hard work!

Well, that's me, isn't it, Robbie wrote to Rebecca. *Dear blank. That's just how I feel at the moment. Totally blank and miserable. I haven't shown the actual letter to anyone else, but you might as well see what a failure I am. Do what you like with it. It would make a paper dart for instance, or might be useful for standing teacups on.*

I'm looking forward to getting back to school, just to get away from Dad! He accuses me of dementia in applying for Politics and Philosophy at Oxford – and elsewhere, too.

Well, he's right about that; I can't think why it seemed such a good idea at the time. But what really upsets him is that I don't want to be a doctor, like him! Tish may want to but I certainly don't. He wants me to change my applications to the other universities and ask if they'll consider me for Medicine. No fear. I don't think I'll bother to go to university at all, as I can't think what to do.

So Doctor Anderson wanted his son to follow in his footsteps! Robbie was pouring his heart out to Rebecca. He'd never really done that before. Suddenly she understood the odd little remark he'd made to her last term, when the broken bones in her left wrist and forearm had finally knitted together successfully. 'Dull but useful,' Robbie had said, quite startling her. 'Doctors.'

The letter ran to four pages. It ended:

There! Now I feel better to have got all that off my chest. I've videoed your film and Tish is bringing it back to school for you. I'm going to take our copy to show people at Garth. The best bit's the end. It quite cheers me up to look at it. Lucky Rebecca. Your future seems pretty clear-cut. One of these days when you're jetting round the world with some tennis circus and I'm sleeping under newspapers somewhere, remember who taught you to serve! Your loving –
ROBBIE XXXXX

Rebecca read the letter through again and then stuffed everything into her bedside locker for safe keeping. She put out the side-light and shed a tear or two on the pillow before she went to sleep.

Poor Robbie. He was in such a muddle.

But if her own future was really as clear-cut as all that, she ought to rejoice.

Oughtn't she?

Walking over to main school next day, for the first assembly of the new term, she asked Mara's opinion. Mara tended to be very sensitive, very intuitive.

'Rebecca, nothing in this world is clear-cut,' said the Greek girl, her dark brown eyes unfathomable. 'So you will have to wait and see.'

The first days of term were hectic, a foretaste of things to come. The teachers were piling on work now, quite remorselessly it seemed to Rebecca: piling on the pressure! Not only were there several pieces of coursework still outstanding, but all the Fifths faced mock GCSE exams straight after half-term, at the beginning of March. The mocks were a practice run to prepare them for the real exams in the summer term.

The final grades awarded on their General Certificate of Secondary Education depended partly on the coursework they'd been doing since the beginning of the Fourth Year and partly on the summer exams. So obviously the latter were very important. In Rebecca's case her grades in three of her subjects, French, German and Latin, were decided purely by the examination! There was no coursework element in language subjects under the Wessex Board regulations. Presumably people might cheat too much and use a dictionary! Was that the reason?

'Don't think the mocks don't matter and you'll have plenty of time to learn things afterwards,' warned Mr Oppenheimer in biology on Tuesday. 'You won't. We're nearly through the syllabus now. By the time you take your mocks, now they're in March, I'll have taught you everything

I can. If you don't know it by then, you're not going to! The purpose of the mocks is to give you experience of exam conditions, how to time yourself properly and work IN SILENCE!' he barked suddenly at Roberta Jones, who'd been whispering to Debbie Rickard.

'You may pick up one or two weak areas from your mock results,' he concluded, 'and that gives you a chance to revise. But that's all. Don't think you can leave most of the work to next term! Now, let's return once more to the food chain, and I am not referring to Tesco's!'

Rebecca felt nerve-wracked. Mr Oppenheimer tended to have that effect on her.

Next lesson, Latin, came as a positive relief. They were just a small group and she loved Pargie! Mr Pargiter was such a good teacher that everything seemed to sink in and stay there, without your noticing it. He also made you feel clever, as though all things were possible! Today he helped Rebecca with a difficult section of Dido and Aeneas and when she'd worked out the case endings and what belonged where, she had a feeling of deep satisfaction, as if completing a difficult crossword puzzle.

'Lovely, Rebecca. You're going to sail through your mocks at this rate. Just wait till we get started on some Greek next year. Yes, Tish? You look like Aeneas reaching the Entrance to the Underworld!'

'And I feel like it, too,' laughed Tish.

As for French lessons, the planned trip to Paris had added much zest. Monsieur Lafarge, the Div 1 teacher, would be in charge of the party. They sidetracked him into talking about the delights of the French capital whenever they could. As he insisted that these discussions be conducted in French, he probably had the last laugh.

The dates of the trip still weren't finalized. M. Lafarge

was finding it something of a headache sorting them out with his counterpart at Trebizon's twin school in Paris. Something to do with not clashing with a skiing trip.

'I hope it doesn't clash with my music heats!' Sue whispered.

'Oh, Sue, that would be awful!' replied Rebecca. It was so exciting. Mr Barrington, the Director of Music, had entered Sue for the Wessex Young Musician of the Year competition and the first heats were to be held this spring.

'It's already clashed with my hockey tour,' said Josselyn Vining, with a shrug. 'I can't possibly do both.'

Joss was in the England 19—U women's hockey group. And she was only sixteen! As they were going to tour Europe, she should worry, thought Rebecca. She herself started daydreaming, with a sense of pleasurable anticipation, about staying with Emmanuelle. She'd never actually been abroad before, unlike a lot of the Trebizon girls, who seemed to flit about all over the place. It was going to be a real holiday. Wow, she'd certainly need one by the time this term was over!

For, of course, spurred on by the earth-shattering thoughts that Mrs Ericson had put into her head (Number One in her age group – a dream, surely?), tennis loomed large in Rebecca's life. She had some intensive, and very useful, one-to-one coaching with Miss Darling in double games on Wednesday. But most of all she was grateful to Joss. She was so lucky to have someone like Joss Vining at Trebizon.

Effortlessly brilliant at everything she touched, including schoolwork that she seemed to sail through without actually ever doing any, Joss had *really* been England's top junior at one time. Only her temperament and greater interest in hockey had made her decide to give up serious tennis competition. But she was still a formidable opponent and gave Rebecca some excellent games in the lunch hours.

The school's all-weather courts were taken over by net-ball and sometimes hockey (when the pitches were water-logged) in the winter. But the staff court was playable for the weather was cold but not cold enough for frosts. As she slammed the ball all over the court, Rebecca felt her confidence returning by the hour. However, scurrying hither and thither to scoop up balls as they played, she remembered Naomi Cook's offer to act as ball-girl some-times. She might take her up on it! At the same time, she frowned slightly. She was a bit breathless, wasn't she? She was still rather out of condition. She'd join Tish for a run tomorrow. For nearly a year now, Tish's great craze had been distance running. She was up every morning at first light, off down the fire escape, off to pound across the damp misty sands of Trebizon Bay before breakfast.

But Rebecca was getting the measure of Joss once more! These lunchtime games were getting closer by the minute, neck and neck.

By Thursday evening, exhausted, Rebecca lay on her bed to read up some geography. It was peaceful, up here on the attic floor of Court House. Girls were quietly working away in their individual cubicles, the very faintest tinkle of pop music coming from a dozen sets of headphones. In the corner cubicle, on the other side of the door to the fire escape, Tish was writing up some chemistry notes.

Some people were out. Elf and Margot had gone to play table tennis. Sue had taken her violin case and caught the minibus to Garth College. There was Joint Orchestra practice tonight. Mara, who had recently started learning the flute, had gone with her. She wasn't good enough for the orchestra yet but she liked to go along and listen.

Some time during the evening, fully dressed on top of her duvet, Rebecca fell asleep, her geography book slipping from her hand.

The next thing she knew, Sue was waking her up, just back from Garth. She was holding an envelope.

'Wake up, Rebecca!' smiled Sue. 'A note for you. Justy gave it to me to give you. It's from Robbie.'

Justin Thomas, Sue's boyfriend at Garth College, was a friend of Robbie Anderson.

'From Robbie?' Rebecca was startled. 'What's wrong?'

'Don't think anything's wrong,' laughed Sue. 'Justy says Robbie's suddenly got more cheerful. Hadn't you better get into your night things, Rebeck?' And Sue headed across to her own cubicle, yawning with tiredness herself.

Dear Rebecca, said the note. *No, I haven't shot myself. In fact, I've been told something pleasant. I've got my self-respect back. Tear up that miserable screed I sent you. Can I take you out to tea on Sunday? Justy says I can borrow his car. It's not cycling weather, is it.*

Rebecca hastily scribbled a reply.

Dear Robbie. Relieved to hear you're alive and well. Longing to see you. I've got to go to Exonford this Sunday – tennis training. How about Saturday week? The Saturday afternoon? Can I ask Mrs Barry if we can go out to tea then instead? Can you re-book the car!

She'd post it to Robbie first thing in the morning, from the school pillar-box. It was funny, the way they both at the same time didn't feel like using the phone any more. It was as though the things they had to say to each other were too special for their boarding-house payphones, which were public, to say the least. Notes were much better.

Over the next few days she wondered what the 'something pleasant' was that Robbie had been told. She'd hear all about it on Saturday.

In the meantime, she was told something pleasant herself. It wasn't simply pleasant: it was amazing.

FOUR

THE MEREST GLIMPSE

It was after tennis training at Exonford, the county town. Rebecca had been to church in the morning and then spent a gruelling afternoon at the Exonford stadium. After an hour's workout in the gym, she found herself on one of the indoor courts, at the receiving end of a barrage of shots from two members of the senior squad. Then, coaching. She was pleased with her progress and so was Mrs Ericson.

'Good, Rebecca. You're getting fluent again and your forehand's quite formidable. What did they do to you at that hospital! Now go and shower. Come and see me in the office before you leave. I've some interesting news for you.'

Refreshed by her shower, a clean T-shirt under her red county tracksuit, she reported to the county coach as instructed. She was intrigued. What did Mrs Ericson want to see her for?

'Well, Rebecca. Somebody wants to come and watch you play next Sunday. Here. At the Indoor.'

'Watch *me*?' exclaimed Rebecca. An indoor tournament had been arranged for the County Seniors next Sunday and she'd been invited to join them. 'Who, Mrs Ericson? Why?'

'A young woman called Brenda Brogan. She phoned me yesterday and asked permission. She saw you play at Eastbourne. She's coming all the way from London.'

'Why?' Rebecca repeated in amazement. 'Who is she?'

'She works for Herman Lasky. The agent.'

'I've never heard of him!' exclaimed Rebecca.

'There's no reason why you should have done. But he's a very successful agent. He handles, let me see –'

Mrs Ericson reeled off the names of four teenage tennis stars. They were all of them crowd-pullers. All of them rich. All of them glamorous.

'It seems that Mr Lasky might be interested in *you*, Rebecca. Just thought I'd better warn you.'

'Well, thanks,' was all Rebecca could think of to say. What amazing news!

The palms of her hands felt clammy as she picked up her sports bag to leave the office.

'Hurry now, Rebecca. Mind you don't miss your train. See you next Sunday!'

'Rebecca!' yelled a cheerful voice at the railway station, and a boy with spiky hair came bounding up to her. 'How *are* you? Don't tell me they've let you out of prison!'

'Cliff!' laughed Rebecca. She used to go to school with Cliff Haynes in London and they'd recently met up again. His family had moved to the West Country and he attended Caxton High, the local state school. He'd taken Rebecca to a disco there last term. 'What are you doing in Exonford on a wet Sunday afternoon?'

'Been to watch some football,' replied Cliff. 'You?'

'Tennis training,' explained Rebecca. 'I –'

She was about to blurt it out, what Mrs Ericson had told her. But the train was arriving. By the time they'd got on board and Cliff had gone to buy her a can of lemonade at the buffet, she'd collected her thoughts.

There was nothing to tell, yet. It might come to naught. In which case, if she got excited and started telling people, she could look a bit silly, couldn't she? She wouldn't say a word about it to anyone, not even Tish and Co. Better see what happened next Sunday, first.

So as the train rattled back to Trebizon, Rebecca and Cliff talked about their GCSEs and pop music and how they'd spent the Christmas holidays. Cliff obviously hadn't seen the film on Boxing Day, so there was no reason to talk about tennis at all.

But she told Robbie, the following Saturday. She couldn't help herself.

They sat by an upstairs window in the restaurant at Dennizon Point, right on top of the cliffs there.

There was a breathtaking view across the fierce, angry winter sea. A large fishing-boat was pitching and tossing on the horizon. It made Rebecca feel seasick just to look at it.

Robbie was cheerful and relaxed. He was wearing a thick red polo-neck sweater, his dark curly hair all springy on the neck. Tish's was the same way when life was going well. You could always tell if the Andersons were pleased with life, by their hair; or perhaps those were the only times they bothered to wash it!

'The college wrote the most brilliant letter to Dr Simpson,' he explained. It seemed that his headmaster had taken him into his confidence and told him everything that was in the letter. 'They said I was an obvious Oxford candidate and had written outstanding exam papers, but had shown lamentable lack of direction during my interviews. That the courses at the university are very demanding and unlikely to be completed successfully by a student who lacks real interest and motivation. In other words, it's simply not enough to have the brains and want to go there because it seems glamorous. It's not like *Brideshead Revisited* any more. It's a real sweatshop!'

'So they say,' commented Rebecca. 'What else?' she asked eagerly.

'They're suggesting that I sort myself out and re-apply after A levels for a place next year! Take a year off! That's what they seem to be saying. Dr Simpson says it means they probably want me after all, as long as I find something I really want to do.'

'Oh, Robbie, isn't that good!' exclaimed Rebecca.

She didn't ask him if he'd had any ideas yet about what he did want to do. She could tell he hadn't. There was plenty of time for that, now. It was enough to see him happy again.

And so, piling into the cream cakes he'd bought, over-come by a feeling of well-being at being in such a glamorous restaurant, she blurted out her own piece of news.

'Wow!' he said.

'What d'you think it means, Robbie?'

'Maybe this man Lasky is going to offer you a contract! Maybe you're going to be a millionaire!'

'I'd better play well tomorrow then, hadn't I,' she said, trying to sound calm. 'Don't tell anyone, will you, Robbie?'

'Of course I won't. Wow!' he said again. 'What did I tell you, eh?'

As Robbie drove her back to school in Justin's little car, her mind returned to a completely different subject.

Was that Naomi Cook they saw on the way? she wondered.

When they'd left the school grounds earlier, by the back lane, it had been around three o'clock. They'd used the gates by St Mary's, the little church in the grounds, and Robbie had zoomed away up the hill, pleased to be driving again.

They'd passed what Rebecca took to be a local cyclist, flying down the hill from the opposite direction. A small girl wearing old jeans and a denim jacket, head bent over the handlebars of an oversized bike. Rebecca had only caught the merest glimpse of the face.

It was only after she'd gone past that Rebecca had wondered something. Had that been Naomi Cook?

If so, where'd she been? Juniors were forbidden to wear clothes like that when they went out, and they weren't allowed out today, anyway! Surely it couldn't have been Naomi?

She'd then told Robbie all about the First Year girl:

'Her family will be down here by now. I hope she hasn't been nipping home to see them or something,' Rebecca had said, with a worried frown. 'Oh, surely she wouldn't do anything so silly?'

'D'you think that *could* have been Naomi, borrowing a bike and breaking bounds?' she said out loud to Robbie now.

'Search me,' he grunted. 'You know what she looks like, Rebeck. I don't.'

FIVE

THE MYSTERY OF THE MISSING WALKMAN

Sunday again. The whole day at Exonford this time. The Indoor was a round robin tournament. Eight members of the county squads took part: four seniors, two 18–Us and two 16–Us, Rebecca and another girl, Madeleine Marks. In the course of the day, everybody played one long set against everybody else. There were three sets in the morning and four in the afternoon, with good long breaks in between, of course, waiting for courts to come free.

Rebecca played very well indeed.

She got nicely into her stride during the morning and when Brenda Brogan arrived, just at the end of the lunch break, and briefly introduced herself, Rebecca's adrenalin started to flow.

She took the first set of the afternoon 6–4 from one of the 18–Us. She loved the sensation of being totally fit once more. She was glad she'd gone running with Tish every morning this week. It made a difference! But mostly she was exhilarated by the sight of that tall elegant figure in the fur coat, watching her from the shadows.

She reached her peak in the second match of the

afternoon: defeating the county's Number One Ladies Senior player, 10–8, after a long and gritty battle. She sat down afterwards and towelled herself, drinking copiously. When she'd recovered, she noticed that the figure in furs had disappeared.

'Oh, has Miss Brogan gone back to London now?' she asked Mrs Ericson, in obvious disappointment.

'Not at all,' smiled the coach. 'She's just asked if she can use my phone. That was a fine performance, Rebecca. Well done. I shouldn't wonder if she's reporting back to Mr Lasky right now.'

Mrs Ericson had guessed correctly.

The telephone conversation was brief, but to the point.

'Well?'

'She's just beaten the Number One Senior.'

'And saleable?'

'Yes.'

'OK. Give her a lift back to school. Tell her if she has a good start to the season I'm interested.'

'Mr Lasky's definitely interested in you Rebecca,' explained Miss Brogan, as the beautiful silver-grey Porsche zipped through the countryside between Exonford and Trebizon. 'Of course, he can't offer you a contract at this stage.'

'Of course not,' agreed Rebecca, in a total daze.

She'd never been in a car like this before! Leaning back, relaxed, wrapped round in the warmth of the bucket-shaped seat. She could smell its real leather, mingled with the faint fragrance of Miss Brogan's perfume, tangy, exotic, reminiscent of dark blue skies on hot summer nights . . . There was some brilliant music playing softly on the car stereo.

'He'll need to see how you shape up in the next few months. What's your next major tournament? Bristol?'

'Yes, I'm down for that,' said Rebecca eagerly.

'Good. You can count on Mr Lasky coming to Bristol in person. You'll be the second young player he'll be watching there.'

'When – when will he decide?' Rebecca wanted to know.

'After the Prudential at Easter, most likely. He'd have to consult with your parents, of course,' replied Brenda Brogan. 'Have you got GCSEs this summer?'

'Yes.'

'Well, obviously you'd have to stay on at school to finish those. And you're sixteen in July?'

'How did you know that?' exclaimed Rebecca in surprise.

'From the rankings sheet, of course!' laughed Miss Brogan. 'Well, Mr Lasky will come close to a decision at Bristol and then take a *final* decision at Easter, after the Prudential. That way your parents can give your school the usual term's notice. So you'd be free to leave at the end of the summer term. Straight into a contract with the best agent in the country! He'd fix you up with a coach, sponsorship deals, everything! And more tennis and more money than you've ever dreamed of, Rebecca!'

Rebecca leaned back on the head-rest and watched clouds and tree-tops whizzing by. Her scalp was tingling and she felt very slightly faint. So . . . if she played superbly well in the next few weeks, everything could happen with dizzying speed. Much faster than she'd ever dreamt; much faster than she'd ever planned. She'd leave school and turn professional this summer! She'd be playing tennis full time, with her own coach and wonderful clothes and Mr Lasky would get her sponsorships! She'd go to Eastbourne this summer as a pro. There'd be a car to drive her around. No more transport problems! Not like last summer when Mum and Dad had to hang around in the rain, not enjoying their 'little holiday' at Eastbourne one bit and glad when it was all over – even though she'd nearly reached the semi-finals!

Finally she said, in a subdued voice:

'My parents are out of the country. They work in Saudi Arabia.'

Miss Brogan swung the car off the main road as she saw the signs for Trebizon. She gave Rebecca a sidelong glance.

'Oh, that's a pity.'

'They'll be back in the summer!' Rebecca quickly explained. 'The beginning of July. They'll be back home on leave for two months.'

'Ah.' Miss Brogan gave a quick nod. 'That's all right, then. Nothing would have to be signed before July. But of course we shall need to sound out their opinion, long before then. Mr Lasky will want to write to them and give them some idea of what's in his mind.'

'I'll write to them, as well!' Rebecca exclaimed.

'Good. Now, where are we? Can you give me directions, Rebecca?'

As the school gates came in sight, all Rebecca could think of was the car – and how glamorous Miss Brogan looked. She checked her watch. Nearly time for the Sunday evening TV Serial – the Agatha Christie! Rebecca and friends, 'the six', were all hooked on that at the moment. With luck, Tish and Sue and Co. would be crowding into the common room just as she got back.

They'd be downstairs and they'd see the car arrive! They'd see her step out of the car. What a surprise it was going to give them. And then she'd tell them her amazing news. At last she had something solid to tell them! Solid, but not definite.

The car scrunched to a halt in front of Court House.

'Now, Rebecca,' said Miss Brogan, reaching for her handbag, 'if you could just give me your parents' address.'

Rebecca glanced through the passenger window, towards the common room. A few flakes of snow were falling. Surely one of her friends would look out at any moment and spot the car! One was always interested when cars rolled up at Court House, especially if they looked like this one!

Keeping half an eye on the front of the building, Rebecca recited the address while the woman wrote it down carefully in a notebook. Sure enough, two faces had appeared at the common room window. But they were just a couple of Fourth Years, Belinda Burridge and Wanda Gorski. No sign of her friends. Oh, come on! Surely they'd all come crowding to the window, now that she'd been spotted?

'Right.' Miss Brogan snapped her notebook shut. 'Must dash. It's a long drive back to London.' She leaned across and opened the passenger door, giving Rebecca a warm smile. 'Off you go, then. It's up to you now! No promises. Nothing definite – not yet. But everything to work for, Rebecca!'

As the car disappeared from view, Rebecca turned away feeling empty and walked through the snowflakes to the front door, carrying her sports grip. She felt a silly pang of disappointment that her friends hadn't seen the car, after all.

She looked into the common room. The TV serial was just beginning.

'Who was that?' asked Belinda.

'What a fantastic car!' exclaimed Wanda.

'Just a lift, that's all,' said Rebecca, quickly withdrawing.

Nobody in there. Where *were* they? It wasn't like them to miss the serial!

She raced upstairs towards the Fifth Year quarters on the top floor.

There they were – on the top landing! They were all in a huddle, talking to someone. Something was going on.

'Hiya! I'm back!' she called out excitedly, powering up the last flight of stairs.

But none of them turned round; they were too busy talking to have heard her.

There seemed to be a rival attraction.

As Rebecca reached the top landing, she saw who was the centre of all the attention.

It was Holly Thomas.

Sue Murdoch tended to feel slightly responsible for Justin's little sister, mainly because Justin always wanted to hear news of her when they met. Holly was a Second Year now. Although she'd settled in quite nicely at Trebizon, after the dramas of the previous summer, she still tended to be accident-prone. Everything always happened to Holly!

Rebecca could see now that her face was badly tear-stained. However, the fact that she was holding Tish's old cassette recorder in her arms, the one which Tish had had since the Second Year, seemed to be cheering her up.

'May I *really* borrow it, Tish?' she was saying.

'Yes, yes,' said Tish. 'I keep telling you! There's nowhere to fit headphones. We're not allowed them up here without headphones! Fifth Year rules. It's duff! It's useless!'

Rebecca smiled in surprise, remembering how pleased Tish had been with it, at Holly's age.

'Shoo, now!' Sue was saying. 'Time to get back to Juniper! Miss Morgan will be wondering where you are. And we're going to miss our serial! Rebeck! You're back!'

'What about your action committee?' Holly was

protesting as they bundled her downstairs. 'You're good at solving mysteries!'

'Too busy for Action Committee!' scolded Mara. 'We've got our GCSEs to think about. You will have to form one of your own, Holly!'

Rebecca dumped her sports bag on the landing and doubled back down, to join them.

'Being generous, aren't you, Tish?' she whispered. 'What's going on?'

'Somebody's pinched Holly's Walkman. It's walked! It's brand new. She got it for Christmas. She left it on the table downstairs at Juniper, over the weekend, sometime. Now it's definitely gone.'

'That's awful,' said Rebecca. 'But guess what, I've got some news too! I can't wait to tell you!'

And so as Holly left the building, Rebecca sat at the bottom of the stairs, with her friends gathered round her, and told them what there was to tell.

After that, the mystery of the missing Walkman faded into insignificance.

Somebody was interested in Rebecca! An agent! The one who managed all the famous teenage stars!

Rebecca had a contract in the offing! She might be good enough to turn pro this summer. She'd be rich. She'd be famous. She'd have to leave Trebizon . . .

How had the agent noticed her? He must have seen the film, that was it. Yes, surely, that must have been it . . .

What a shame they missed seeing the woman and the Porsche! Never mind, they'd be seeing them both again sometime, by the sound of it.

They were several minutes late for the Agatha Christie. There'd been another murder at the vicarage, apparently. Three corpses in one evening!

SIX

A BAD SIGN

Rebecca yawned through lessons on Monday morning. It was not so much the physically tiring day at Exonford, but the fact that she'd then stayed up late scribbling letters: to Robbie, to her grandmother and then to Cliff. She wanted to share her news with them as quickly as possible. They'd all be thrilled, in their different ways!

The letter to her parents would take a bit more thought, so she'd put that off for a while. She wasn't sure whether they'd be pleased or not.

Also she decided she didn't want it filtering through to the staff at Trebizon, not even Mrs Barrington, her house-mistress. Not yet. She'd sworn the rest of 'the six' to secrecy.

After all, it wasn't definite.

As if all this activity weren't enough, or perhaps because it was too much, Rebecca hadn't been able to get to sleep for ages. She lay looking up at the skylight above her bed, at that square of darkness, wondering if there might be more snow during the night. There'd only been a few flurries so far. She'd fixed up a game with Joss tomorrow lunch hour. If it snowed they wouldn't be able to play! she fretted.

No wonder Rebecca was tired the next morning. She got ticked off in German for not paying attention. She'd been staring dreamily through the window, realizing that snow clouds had moved away to be replaced by wintry sunshine. Good! The court would be playable . . .

Her thoughts were turning to Naomi Cook. It would be nice to have someone pick up balls today. She'd offered, hadn't she? Why not take her up on it?

Not only that. It would be a chance to talk to her. To probe a bit. Rebecca had been worrying about the First Year girl and the fact that she might be breaking bounds. There was something not quite right about the whole set-up with Naomi, something odd. Rebecca had sensed it. Tish and Sue had been sweet to Holly. Well, maybe Naomi needed a bit of kindness, too. If she were doing daft things like popping home, the sooner she stopped it the better, before she was found out!

'Rebecca, for the last time, please give me the Dative!' exploded Herr Fischer.

At lunchtime, in her quiet way, Naomi seemed pleased to come and ball-girl for Rebecca and Joss. She obviously hadn't planned on doing anything else. Still no particular friends, Rebecca noted.

But it was a godsend not have to pick up the balls today!

Joss gave her a wonderful game. Rebecca won, 7–6. Possibly.

When Joss had gone, Rebecca stayed behind on the pretext of seeing to the net and told Naomi she wanted to talk to her.

'Can I tell you something first?' asked Naomi, collecting up the last two balls and putting them in the box.

'Of course,' said Rebecca, in surprise.

Naomi came across with the box. Her cheeks were paler than usual. She was having to summon up her courage. She didn't want to upset Rebecca! Maybe Rebecca wouldn't ask her to come again.

'Well?' she prompted. The First Year girl had suddenly become tongue-tied. 'What is it?'

'You didn't win!' Naomi blurted out.

Rebecca felt angry and at the same time dismayed, by her own anger!

'What on earth d'you mean?'

'That last shot Joss did – you said it was out. But it just touched the line. I saw it!'

'Oh.' Rebecca was slightly appalled. 'Are you sure?'

'Positive.'

'Oh. I made a mistake then. I'll tell Joss later.' Then she added: 'Thanks for telling me.'

Once again, she had to hand it to Naomi. She was certainly honest!

'Your family's moved down here now, then?' Rebecca asked casually, as they left the court. 'Do you feel it makes any difference?'

'Well –' Naomi gave her a guarded look. 'It's better knowing they're not far away. Of course, I can't see anybody or anything. But they'll be able to come to things. I mean, supposing I get in the netball team. And it won't be far to go home, at half-term, will it? But I wish . . .'

She broke off, looking unutterably sad.

'There *do* have to be rules,' said Rebecca, as gently as she could. 'There are hardly any day-girls. Miss Welbeck doesn't like having them. Because it *is* a boarding school. And if boarders who had families living quite near could pop home when they wanted, it would be unsettling for everyone else, wouldn't it? I mean, me, for instance.' She smiled. 'My parents are in Saudi Arabia.'

'Oh, it's not that I'm homesick, it's not like that,' said Naomi, awkwardly. 'I'm not a baby. It's just that –'

She stopped, unable to continue; clearly overcome with emotion.

Rebecca waited, hoping that she *would* continue. But as the moments passed it was obvious that she wasn't going to. And Rebecca knew that she couldn't intrude on something that was obviously very private.

But there was one thing that had to be sorted out and she decided to take the plunge:

'Naomi. Did I see you on Saturday afternoon?' she asked, meaningfully.

Naomi's face immediately became slightly brighter.

'You might have done!' she said. 'At netball practice, you mean? Did you? Was I any good?'

'I –' Rebecca was nonplussed.

'I'm only a reserve at the moment,' said Naomi. 'But Jay Larcombe, she's First Year Head of Games, you know, she says I'm to come to practices every Saturday and if I improve, I might make the First Year team.'

'That's good, isn't it, Naomi?' said Rebecca in relief.

She knew the times of those junior netball practices. They took place on a Saturday, from two till four in the afternoon. So she'd been mistaken! How silly she'd been.

It hadn't been Naomi out on that bike, after all.

'Couldn't matter less,' said Joss with a shrug, when Rebecca apologized, just before French lesson.

'I just don't know what made me feel so certain you'd hit it out,' confessed Rebecca.

'Because you so badly wanted it to be out, that's why,'

laughed Joss. 'I was pretty sure myself the ball was in. It didn't matter. But I thought it was a bad sign. It means the pressure's getting to you, Rebecca. Tennis is like that.'

'What, you mean you can convince *yourself*? See things out when they're in and vice versa?'

'Some people can. Don't get like that, Rebecca. Remember, I've been there, babe!'

'Oh, don't be silly, Joss,' laughed Rebecca, uncomfortably. 'I just made a mistake, that's all.'

She'd been wondering whether to let Joss into her secret or not. She liked Joss. But now she decided she wouldn't.

She went into French, hoping that the dates for the trip to Paris had been fixed by now. She'd had a lovely long letter from Emmanuelle in the post this morning!

No luck. At the French end, they still hadn't got their act together.

Sometime on the following Saturday, nobody could be quite sure when, something else was stolen from Juniper House. Jay Larcombe's brand-new Trebizon blazer, of all things.

It had been hanging in her wardrobe, in the dormitory upstairs. When she went to put it on to go to church, first thing on Sunday morning, it had vanished!

The previous weekend, when Holly Thomas's Walkman had gone, Miss Morgan had finally reached the conclusion (after the building had been thoroughly searched) that somebody from outside the school had nipped in and taken it, a delivery boy perhaps.

'After all, Holly, it was very careless of you to leave it on the table in the hall, just by the main door,' the junior school housemistress had scolded. 'Anybody passing, over the weekend, might have seen it and been tempted. I've given the police all the details but they say the best you can hope for now is that one of their men will spot it in a second-hand shop.'

But now the disappearance of the blazer put things in a slightly different light. It would have been difficult for some outside person to have sneaked around the dormitories upstairs without being seen, even supposing such a person wanted to steal a school blazer! They'd have had to pass Miss Morgan's office, for a start, and matron or one of the assistant matrons were always around, apart from the scores of junior girls who tended to mill around the big building at weekends.

'I tell you, it's an inside job – my Walkman, too!' Holly said excitedly to Sue and some of the others, bumping into them at the sports centre on the Sunday afternoon. 'There's a thief in Juniper House! Well, we're going to do what you suggested, Mara. We're going to form an action committee of our own.' She turned to her friend, Harriet. 'Aren't we, Harri?'

'Yes! Sara Butters wants to be in it, too!'

'Who'd want to pinch a blazer?' commented Tish.

'Couldn't somebody have taken it by mistake?' suggested Sue.

'Definitely not! Matron's made everyone turn their things out to see if they've got it. It took all morning! And they haven't. She's looked.'

'Someone's pinched it and they've hidden it somewhere!' added Harriet. 'But we've had a brilliant idea, how to catch them. Haven't we, Holly?'

'Yes.'

Rebecca missed all this.

She was tennis training in Exonford again, dreaming

about her future . . . and wondering how on earth she was going to get her maps drawn for geography coursework and handed in by Monday morning.

SEVEN

SETTING A TRAP

'Who on earth would want to pinch Jay Larcombe's blazer?' mused Tish out loud, from the corner cubicle. It was late on Sunday evening and she was lying tracksuited on her bed, bicycling in the air. *Twenty-three . . . twenty-four . . . twenty-five . . .* she counted. 'Any ideas, Rebecca?' she shouted.

Rebecca was sitting at the work-table in her own cubicle, biting her lip and frowning in deep concentration as she tried to make an accurate copy of a map of Australia. It was so fiddly! The light wasn't very good. She needed a brighter bulb in her desk-lamp. She had yet to write all the main towns and cities in – and the lines of latitude and longitude! And it all had to be as neat and accurate and as near to perfection as possible, to go in her coursework folder. Drat! She hadn't left room for Tasmania at the bottom of the page! She'd have to start all over again!

She was tired, tired, tired.

'REBECCA!' Tish cupped her hands to her mouth and yelled over the wall of her cubicle. 'I SAID, GOT ANY IDEAS?'

'No!' Rebecca suddenly screamed. 'I don't know and I

don't care who pinched Jay Larcombe's blazer! I've got to get this *done*.'

All along the central aisle on the top floor of Court House came grunts and groans and winter coughs from the various cubicles. The majority of girls were already in bed.

'Shut up, you two!'

'Some of us want to get some sleep.'

'*I'm* tired!' protested Jenny Brook-Hayes.

At that, Rebecca just ground her teeth. What made Jenny think she wasn't? She was exhausted. She couldn't start all over again.

She wrote Please Turn Over at the bottom of the page and drew Tasmania on the back.

'Sorry for biting your head off last night,' Rebecca whispered to Tish, early next morning, as they tiptoed down the fire escape at first light. They were warmly dressed in tracksuits and scarves, off for the usual workout.

'Sure you shouldn't be getting some more sleep?' asked Tish, sympathetically.

'No. It's going to be a lovely morning.'

The skies were clear and the chilly air had a tang to it as they raced across the beach, scrunching the tiny crystals of frost that gave the dark sands a pale sheen. The tide was far out. They ran right down to the edge of the sea, where the reflected sunrise stained the water purple and silver towards the horizon. They then turned and zigzagged across the wide bay to the headland, pounded up a steep path to the top and then flung themselves down to recover their breath. They leant their backs against a withered tree and stared up at the gradually lightening sky; listening to the cries of the gulls wheeling round Mulberry Cove, which lay below them on the other side of the headland. The seagulls swooped, dived, searching for food, flashes of light in the shadowy cove. A row of them perched on the dark silhouette of a boat.

'I wouldn't mind being a seagull. Free as a bird! It's all too much at the moment,' Rebecca confessed, at last.

'Bad timing,' agreed Tish, tersely.

Tish Anderson found school work fairly effortless, including the punishing GCSE schedule, but even she had decided not to compete in any more big races before the summer; after exams would be soon enough. She was running at the moment for pure enjoyment.

'I've got this crazy idea,' said Rebecca, 'that I want to get all A or B grades on my certificate. Last term, when I didn't have to, couldn't, play any tennis, I realized that it's perfectly possible.'

They got to their feet and slowly descended the tracks, back down into Trebizon Bay. It was quite light now. Soon be time for breakfast.

After a while, glancing at Rebecca, Tish said:

'From what Miss Moneybags had to say, you're not going to need them. Those good grades.'

'Of course I need them!' reacted Rebecca quickly.

'Why?'

'Well . . .' Rebecca faltered. Why had she reacted with such certainty like that? 'I don't know. Insurance, maybe. Supposing I don't make it? Supposing I don't get offered that contract?' She suddenly felt uncertain, confused. 'What really frightens me at the moment, Tish, is that I might just end up a general failure. Rotten GCSEs, because of all the tennis. Then not getting the tennis contract because I haven't worked hard enough because of the GCSEs . . .'

'You'll have to put one of them first then,' said Tish.

'In that case, it had better be the tennis,' decided Rebecca.

Tish bent down to tie up one of the laces on her trainers. Without looking up, she said, quite casually: 'I expect you'll make it. We'd all miss you, you know.'

Rebecca swallowed hard. And she'd miss them! It didn't bear thinking about. 'It's got to happen first,' she said quickly. 'Come on, Tish, race you back to school.'

The same day, in Latin, Pargie questioned them all about their A level forms.

They'd been asked to take these forms home during the Christmas holidays and give the whole matter careful thought: which three subjects they wished to specialize in at Advanced Level, when they went into the Lower Sixth next year.

Miss Welbeck, the principal, liked to have these forms in by the middle of the Fifth year, giving her staff plenty of time to plan their Sixth Form teaching groups. It was very difficult sometimes to sort out a timetable that gave every girl her first choice of subjects, without any of them clashing. It could be quite a headache.

Mrs Devenshire, the school secretary, had complained that some of the forms were very late in coming in.

'Remember that they *must* be in by half-term,' Mr Pargiter reminded them. 'That's the final deadline. Rebecca, are you sorted out?'

'Oh, yes!' she said happily. 'I handed mine in the first day of term. I want to do French, history and Latin – and GCSE Greek, or maybe GCSE Russian, if that's possible.'

Tish gave her a very strange look.

Although Rebecca didn't realize it, her coach at school knew her secret. Mrs Ericson had confided to Greta Darling that there might well be a contract in the offing, if Rebecca did well at Bristol at half-term and equally well at Edgbaston after Easter. But of course it wasn't to be talked about yet. As far as Mrs Ericson knew, Rebecca's parents had yet to be consulted.

Miss Darling felt a deep sense of pleasure on hearing this news but had no difficulty in concealing her emotions. The Wimbledon umpire and ex-Wightman Cup player, grey-haired and ramrod-backed, rarely smiled. She coached Rebecca as usual on the Wednesday afternoon, in the gym this time because it was sleeting outside.

'The weather's supposed to warm up by the weekend,' she informed Rebecca casually, 'so I've fixed up a game for you with Catherine Wright. She says she'll drive over here on Saturday afternoon, weather permitting. I gather you both fought like tigers at the Indoor.'

'Catherine Wright?' began Rebecca, eagerly. That was the name of the county's number one senior. 'I'd like that – oh . . .'

'What's the matter?' asked her coach, seeing the worried frown.

'I've got a lot of prep for Saturday –'

'Then you must do it on Sunday. I'll ask Mrs Ericson if you can be excused tennis training this Sunday, just for once. I think this would be better for you!'

'Thanks!' said Rebecca, in relief.

She looked forward to Saturday's match and watched the weather anxiously. By Friday the skies had cleared and she spent the lunch hour practising her service. It looked as though the staff court would be playable tomorrow!

'I'll umpire,' Miss Darling said to her in the dining-hall at

51

lunchtime on Saturday. 'Find a couple of juniors to ball-girl, will you?'

Rebecca immediately thought of Naomi.

Carrying her rackets, sweater and tracksuit on over her tennis things, she hurried over to Juniper House immediately after lunch.

At the main entrance to the junior boarding house she caught hold of someone just coming out with a skipping-rope. 'Could you find Naomi Cook for me, please?'

'Yes, Rebecca!' said the girl eagerly. 'I know where she is. She's upstairs.'

While the junior went to find Naomi, Rebecca came inside and loitered in the hall. It was chilly waiting outside! She'd ask Naomi to find someone to partner her as ball-girl; she'd let her choose . . .

As Rebecca leant against the oak hall table, she smiled to see a box of chocolates sitting there, still in its cellophane wrapper. It was a vaguely surprising sight – unopened chocolates in Juniper House, what a paradox! Simultaneously she became conscious of suppressed giggling and 'Ssshh'-ing noises. Staring at some heavy, velvet, floor-length curtains behind the main door, she noticed that they were bulging rather strangely and two pairs of feet were sticking out underneath!

Some juniors hiding. Who were they hiding from? she wondered idly. Then Naomi appeared on the stairs.

'Emma says you want me for something!' she said with pleasure. She was holding a plastic carrier bag. 'You've only just caught me, Rebecca!'

'I was just wondering, Naomi, if – '

She broke off. Naomi was in casual clothes, jeans and a sweater, but bulging out of the top of the carrier bag were her school tracksuit and trainers.

Of course, it was Saturday afternoon!

'How silly of me. You've got netball practice!'

'Oh, you wanted me to ball-girl!' said Naomi, noting Rebecca's tennis rackets, disappointed.

'Sorry,' smiled Rebecca. 'I forgot. Never mind.'

She walked with Naomi as far as the sports centre, where the First Year netball players would be convening at around two o'clock. There Rebecca found two Second Years with nothing to do, grabbed them and went off to the staff court to play her match.

It was a great game. Afterwards, Rebecca emerged from a cubicle at the sports centre, glowing pleasurably. She'd had a hot shower and washed her hair. Now, tracksuited again, she towelled her hair vigorously and looked around for a hair-drier.

It had been a wonderfully stretching afternoon! They'd played three sets, but she'd beaten the county number one quite decisively in the final set, 6–3. She was really getting into her stride now. She was playing as well as she'd played last summer. Getting into top form in time for Bristol!

She wandered through to the next lot of showers.

'Anyone seen a hair-drier?' she called out cheerfully.

Then she stopped in her tracks. There was a commotion going on.

'Let go of me!' Naomi Cook was shouting at Holly Thomas, who was dragging her out of one of the shower cubicles only half-way back into her jeans and sweater. 'Let me get my bag!'

'We're going to search your bag first!' said Holly. 'We know what's in it!'

As Rebecca looked on in amazement, Holly's friend

Harriet appeared from the shower cubicle clutching Naomi's plastic carrier bag, stuffed full of sports clothes.

'I've got it, Hol!'

'You're mad!' yelled Naomi angrily, trying to lunge free.

'WHAT on earth is going on?' demanded Rebecca.

The three juniors froze. Then slowly Holly Thomas turned round.

'Rebecca, you can be a witness!' She was still hanging on to Naomi's arm. 'We set a trap. We've got her now! We've caught the person who's been pinching things.'

'We put some chocolates out, to catch the thief!' explained Harriet. 'May Ling saw her take them. She's only just told us, five minutes ago. She saw her put them in this bag, just before netball practice.'

'I don't believe it!' exclaimed Rebecca, advancing. She whisked the bag away from Harriet. 'Leave Naomi's things alone and kindly listen to me.'

EIGHT

PROBLEMS OF HER OWN

'So it was *your* feet I saw sticking out from under the curtains!' said Rebecca. 'Well, I can tell you Naomi didn't put *anything* in her bag before netball practice, certainly not that box of chocolates! I should know. You mean the ones that were on the hall table in Juniper?'

'We came out together, didn't we, Rebecca?' said Naomi, looking relieved. 'I didn't even *see* any chocolates,' she added indignantly.

That look of innocent indignation was good enough for Rebecca, not that she'd needed convincing.

'You don't understand, Rebecca,' Holly was saying impatiently. Her eyes were fixed on the bulging carrier bag that Rebecca now hugged securely under one arm. 'We know Naomi didn't take them *then*. We were watching you, weren't we? But after you'd gone we went off to the toilet for a few minutes – I know it was stupid of us to go off together, wasn't it, Harri? But anyway, when we got back –'

'The box of chocolates had been pinched!' finished Harriet.

'By which time Naomi was over at the sports centre,

getting ready for netball practice,' Rebecca said drily. 'So what's all this silly nonsense about May Ling seeing her?'

It seemed the two Second Year girls had been asking around all afternoon about the chocolates. Without success. Until five minutes ago, when they'd met May Ling coming out of the Hilary Camberwell Music School.

May Ling was Chinese and the youngest girl in the school. Her family had only arrived in England the previous summer. She was strongly tipped to win the Hilary Camberwell Music Scholarship this term.

'May saw Naomi putting the chocolates into that carrier bag!' said Holly triumphantly. 'She was at the top of the stairs, at about two o'clock, leaving Juniper to come to the Hilary. She just thought they must belong to Naomi.'

'It was definitely her, she *saw* her!' echoed Harriet. 'Naomi must have noticed them when you both walked past! Easy enough for her to slip back from the sports centre and get them! She had plenty of time before netball practice!'

Naomi just stood there, open-mouthed.

'So you've got it all sorted out, have you?' said Rebecca, cuttingly. 'Neither of you has stopped for one moment and wondered if May Ling could have been mistaken? We'll see, shall we —'

So saying, she tipped the carrier bag upside down and let its contents spill out on the floor. Angrily. An act of total and absolute faith in Naomi.

Tracksuit bottoms; tracksuit top; training shoes; dirty socks.

No chocolates.

Naomi hurried forward and scrabbled on the floor, stuffing everything back into the bag, embarrassed by the dirty socks.

Holly and Harriet looked uneasy.

'She could have hidden them somewhere –' said Harriet, falteringly.

'Will you please shut up?' said Rebecca.

'But May saw –'

'Listen.' Rebecca walked over and grabbed both girls by their blazer collars. 'If you'd only been in Hong Kong a few months and you saw a Chinese girl from the top of a flight of stairs, dark hair, high cheekbones, couldn't you make a mistake? Mightn't they all look a bit similar to you?'

They fell silent.

'May Ling can't have sorted everyone in Juniper House out yet. All you've got so far is the fact that there's somebody in Juniper who's fair-haired, about five foot tall and likes chocolates. That gives you about fifty girls to choose from. It may be the same person who likes blazers and Walkmans. On the other hand, it may not be. In the meantime, it might be a good idea to apologize to Naomi.'

'Sorry, Naomi,' mumbled Holly.

'Sorry, we thought –' began Harriet.

But Naomi wasn't waiting. Bag in hand, zipping up her jeans as she went, she raced out of the changing rooms, looking tearful.

Sadly Rebecca watched her go. An odd girl out. She almost invited suspicion. When, if ever, was she going to settle down at Trebizon? She could certainly have done without this!

'Go and tell May she got it wrong,' she told the Second Years. 'Before any silly rumours start flying about. Off you go, shoo!'

Rebecca ate a hearty tea with her friends, revelling in the thought of the weekend stretching ahead of her. No tennis training! She owed Emmanuelle a letter. She had a stack of school work to do. She was falling behind again, no doubt about that. Some of her marks were going downhill. But first, something urgent. Something she'd kept on putting off but it had to be done!

She must write that letter to her parents.

She went over to the library in old school to write it; it was so peaceful there. It was the original library, dating right back to the days when 'Trebizon' had been a local noble-man's manor house. The walls were lined with bookshelves of dark mahogany, stretching up the ornately corniced ceilings. The huge latticed windows, with their deep bays and velvet-cushioned window seats, looked out over the deer park at the front of main school.

Rebecca made two false starts with the letter, tore them up and finally decided on the casual approach:

> *Dear Mum and Dad,*
>   *Thanks for your lovely letter with all your news; I got it last week. I've had some very exciting news myself, though perhaps you know about it already. I wonder if Mr Lasky has written to you yet . . .*

And so on. Then she wrote to her French pen-friend.

On Sunday, she rushed through all her prep, hoping to have time for some revision as well. Mocks were after half-term!

Robbie cycled over to see her in the afternoon, a lovely surprise.

'I've been trying to get over to see you ever since I had your letter, Rebeck. I'm getting roped in for rugby again, now Oxbridge is over. So there *was* a contract in the offing? I was right!'

Robbie still hadn't sorted his future out; in fact, he

seemed to have put the future out of his mind. He was concerned about the present and working maniacally for his A levels, so he couldn't stay long.

The same evening, she had a phone call from Cliff and they talked for quite a long time. He'd received her letter but was surprisingly cautious about the idea of her becoming a full-time tennis player: 'It's all right, unless you have another car accident, Rebecca! Anyway, when am I going to see you?'

'I'll be around at half-term!' Rebecca suddenly realized. 'At least, I'll be back here before the others. I shan't be going to Gran's because of Bristol, you see. I'll come straight back here when it's over. But I'll still be on holiday! I'll ask Mrs Barry if you can come and have lunch with us.'

'Yum. Lovely. Is she a good cook?'

'Very.'

Rebecca came off the phone feeling happy. It would be so nice to see Cliff again. She'd go and fix it up with Mrs Barry right away, before she forgot. Then she could phone Cliff back and make it definite.

She hadn't managed to get any revision done, after all.

Late on Tuesday evening, in the little kitchen at the top of Court House, Tish and Sue cornered Rebecca at cocoa time and tackled her about something.

Holly Thomas had been taking Sue into her confidence.

'She's really smarting over this business of the choc-olates,' explained Sue. 'She says you haven't been fair.'

'Naomi Cook's honest,' said Rebecca flatly. 'I told them to go and see May Ling and tell her she'd made a mistake.'

'They did. And May told them she hadn't!'

'All that stuff you gave them about May being Chinese, Rebeck. It just won't wash,' added Tish. 'They've now

59

discovered that Naomi and May are both in One Alpha and even sit together in some lessons!'

'Really?' Rebecca was startled.

Was it possible? Could Naomi have slipped back from the sports centre and stolen those chocolates? She *had* had enough time. Had she taken the blazer . . . and Holly's new Walkman, as well?

No. It was unthinkable.

'Naomi wouldn't pinch anything,' said Rebecca, stubbornly. 'She's not the type. I'd stake my life on that!'

'Oh, Rebeck, no one's asking you to do that!' grinned Tish.

'But Holly wants you to come and talk to May Ling yourself, Rebecca,' said Sue, worriedly. 'They've kept completely quiet about this, because you asked them to. It hasn't been easy! They've had to let May join their action committee for a start.'

'The price of her silence!' added Tish.

'Oh, all right, then,' said Rebecca reluctantly. 'I'll meet them.'

The meeting took place in Moffatt's, the school tuckshop, the next afternoon, straight after Wednesday games. Rebecca arrived from Miss Darling's tennis coaching feeling hot and dishevelled. As if she hadn't got enough to think about! There were the four juniors at the big corner table, all looking very solemn. Holly, Harriet, Sara Butters – and new recruit, May Ling. The junior school 'action committee', modelled on Tish's.

Rebecca bought lemonades all round, then another one for Sue, who arrived late. Tish had said she was too busy to come.

'Naomi's family hasn't got any money,' said Holly. 'That's the first thing.'

'Then they must be very honest, mustn't they?' countered Rebecca. 'Or surely they'd have got hold of some by now.'

'She *hates* her old second-hand blazer, point number two. So she could have been tempted by Jay's.'

'In that case, why isn't she wearing it?' replied Rebecca. 'She's only got to change the nametape. Why's she still wearing that old one?'

'*And* point number three, she hasn't got a Walkman!' insisted Holly, refusing to be put off.

'Neither have I,' laughed Rebecca. 'What does that prove? Anyway, you're suggesting that she *has* got one now. Yours. So where is it? I expect you've had a good look,' she added, disapprovingly.

The juniors fell silent, looking sheepish.

'You've searched, haven't you?' guessed Rebecca. 'Looked through all her things, when she's been out? And you've found nothing! Not one scrap of evidence to support this.'

'But May's positive –' began Harriet.

Rebecca fixed the little Chinese girl with a stern gaze.

'You *thought* it was Naomi taking the chocolates. But from the top of the stairs in Juniper House, you couldn't possibly be sure. When you first said this, it was all quite casual and you thought they were Naomi's own chocolates anyway. But now, as you know, it's much more serious. We're talking about someone being a thief. That's very serious indeed, isn't it? You have to be quite sure, May. You have to be completely positive. Because yours is the only scrap of evidence. *Are* you that positive?'

'I – I don't know,' said the little Chinese girl, frowning, becoming confused. 'I thought it was Naomi, it looked like her. But the face, well maybe . . . maybe it wasn't Naomi's expression . . .'

'There,' said Rebecca, in some relief. 'You're not really sure at all, are you? So that's an end to it. No more nonsense about Naomi, please. You'll have to start all over again.'

'How?' asked Holly, looking depressed. Who'd have dreamt that May would change her mind, just like that! She'd been so certain before! 'How can we, Rebecca? We can't afford to buy any more chocolates.'

'It's horrible there being a thief in Juniper!' interrupted Sara Butters. 'And Hol wants her Walkman back!'

Rebecca and Sue exchanged glances, then nodded to each other.

'Look,' Rebecca said gently, 'we'll help you.'

'The senior Action Committee!' agreed Sue.

'I'll think of something really good,' promised Rebecca. 'After half-term. I'm busy till then. We'll all club together, won't we, Sue? We'll come up with some really tempting bait that no thief could resist.'

'That's right,' added Sue. 'We'll set another trap.'

They got up to go and Holly followed them to the door, looking much happier.

'You promise, Rebecca? You won't forget?'

'Of course I won't, Holly. I'll think of something after half-term. And we'll all keep watch till we catch the thief! That's a solemn promise.'

She meant it. Not just for Holly's sake, but for Naomi's, too.

Poor Naomi. She'd clear this one up, once and for all!

As they walked across to Court House, Sue said: 'You've really cheered them up, Rebecca. You handled it brilliantly! I can't wait to tell Justy the whole thing!'

But Rebecca's mind was already elsewhere.

She had problems of her own, hadn't she.

NINE

THE PRESSURE IS ON

It was the session with Pargie in the morning that had upset Rebecca most of all.

Of course, the frowns coming from Miss Hort's direction lately, after she'd pulled up in maths so well last term, weren't exactly thrilling. And Herr Fischer wasn't too pleased with her, either.

But Pargie! She did like him. And she knew she should have been learning more Latin vocabulary, the difficult words, the ones they'd be getting in GCSE this summer. So it was hardly surprising that the unseen translation she'd done in Monday's lesson contained serious blunders.

'I thought this must have been somebody else's work when I marked it, Rebecca,' said the good-looking, affable young classics teacher.

The words were mildly spoken but they cut Rebecca to the quick. She felt close to tears as patiently, reproachfully, he went through several words that she'd misconstrued in the translation, making a nonsense of it.

'You've got great flair for handling a highly structured language,' he concluded, 'but I had no idea you were so

63

helpless without the dictionary. You can't just guess at the meaning of words, you need to have learnt them.' Mr Pargiter, who had a private pilot's licence and occasionally used flying analogies, added: 'And you're hoping to do some Greek or Russian next year! You can't just play around with languages like these, Rebecca. You can't fly them by the seat of your pants! There are no short cuts to excellence, I'm afraid.'

Tish, head down at the next desk, covertly tried to read Rebecca's expression.

That night Rebecca lay awake, staring up through her skylight at the night sky and the stars twinkling down at her. She sighed.

At this rate, she wasn't going to do well in the mocks. Nor was she going to get those A and B grades in the summer. Not a hope.

Bristol was only ten days away! The pace was hotting up.

This weekend would be entirely taken up with tennis. Miss Darling was driving her to the covered courts in the next county on Saturday, for an inter-county winter fixture: a senior one! They'd be away all day. ('The Dread' being a darling, as Tish would say.) The county selectors had put Rebecca in the senior squad at Number Two to Catherine Wright! It would earn valuable points for her next computer ranking, as well as for the Edgbaston entry form which had to go off after half-term.

Then on Sunday she had to go to Exonford again: Mrs Ericson insisted on it. It would be the last tennis training before Bristol.

And all next week she had matches fixed up at school, weather permitting. Against Joss, against Alison Hissup (the school's Head of Games this year and a good player) and against tough, battling old Mrs Doubleday – the national Women's Institute champion who lived in the town and who was always pleased to give Rebecca some exhausting practice.

On the Friday, school would disperse for half-term. Mrs Barrington would take charge of Rebecca for the Bristol tournament, just as she'd done last year. She'd deliver Rebecca to Great-Aunt Ivy's house in nearby Bath on the Friday evening, stay with an old schoolfriend in the same city and dutifully chauffeuse Rebecca to the tournament and back each day.

Mr Lasky was going to be there, watching her! Mr Lasky was going to be at Bristol, in person!

He'd come close to a decision then, Miss Brogan had said, whether to offer her a contract or not. After that, there was just Edgbaston: and all would be decided.

So she had to do well at Bristol; it was vital.

You have to decide priorities, what to put first, Tish had pointed out to her. School work or tennis? And Rebecca had decided on the tennis, hadn't she.

So it was no use fretting about what Mr Pargiter had said. It was no use fretting about her maths. It was no use fretting about any of it.

If she wanted that tennis contract then everything else had to take second place.

'Just accept you can't do everything,' Rebecca resolved to herself that night, before she fell asleep. 'You've got to be prepared to give other things up. Even if they seem important, too. Even if it hurts to give them up.'

And that, as it turned out, included Paris.

Rebecca performed brilliantly at the inter-county winter fixture, but on the day before they broke up for half-term,

M. Lafarge came into the Div I French lesson with a beaming smile.

'Enfin!' he exclaimed.

He had a piece of paper in his hands.

'All those going on the Paris exchange, now to get your forms out!' he said. 'We have the dates now settled at last. I will read them out, so that you can enter them on your forms. Please take the forms home over half-term for your parents or guardians to sign. Bring them back next Tuesday without fail. I can then book our travel tickets.'

There were rustling noises as everybody looked for their forms. Rebecca got hers out of her folder. She wasn't going to Gran's for half-term! She'd have to post the form for Gran to sign and send back. Mum and Dad knew all about it; they'd agreed.

'Because of their school skiing trip, the dates are later than we first thought. You will be going to Paris right at the end of the Easter holidays. In fact, you will be late back to school. You will all be speaking perfect French, in good time for your GCSE orals!'

M. Lafarge read out the dates.

'Yippee!' whooped Sue softly, in the next desk. 'Just misses my music heats!'

But as Rebecca filled the dates in on her form, a cold, sinking feeling washed through her.

The dates seemed horribly familiar.

When was Edgbaston this year?

As soon as the lesson ended, as her five friends started to converge on her, waving their forms, laughing, joking, she turned and fled.

'Rebecca!'

'What's wrong?'

Her lip trembling, she raced out of main building and

across the grounds to Court House. Up three flights of stairs to the top floor and into Fifth Year quarters, there to streak the whole length of the aisle and dive into her cubicle. Gulping for breath, she gazed at the typewritten tennis schedule on her little notice-board. Surely she couldn't be this unlucky? Surely –

I can't stand it! she thought, almost weeping.

Her friends followed, worried about her.

They found her sitting on her bed, holding the tennis schedule limply in one hand, pale and despondent.

'Oh, Rebeck, *no*?' exclaimed Sue, the first to realize.

'Not Edgbaston?' said Tish.

'Yes, Edgbaston,' said Rebecca, in a dull little voice. 'And I can't miss that, can I? It's the big one, as far as Mr Lasky's concerned. So I won't be able to go to Paris with the rest of you.'

She put a hand over her eyes, fighting back the tears. No French trip! No Emmanuelle! No holiday! No fun! No grade A in her French oral in May! Her shoulders heaved.

The other five were wonderful. They said everything they could think of to cheer her up.

'It's rotten luck but just think of that contract!' said Elf.

'Think how rich you're going to be!' added Margot.

'Famous!' pointed out Mara, though she looked nearly as tearful as Rebecca.

'You'll be able to get us seats at Wimbledon every year –' began Tish.

' – until we're old ladies!' finished Sue.

'We'll boast about you –' Tish did a marvellous imitation of an old crone: 'I used to k-k-know Rebecca Mason when she was j-j-just a girl, before she became a l-l-legend.'

Rebecca managed a weak smile.

'Anyway, just think,' said Elf, in her practical way, 'you'll be jetting all over the world soon. You'll probably be *playing* in Paris in a couple of years' time. Playing at the French Open! Staying in the best hotel!'

'I'd rather just go on the school trip,' said Rebecca, sadly.

The next day, she left for Bath in Mrs Barry's car. Her friends saw her off.

'Got Biffy, Rebeck?'

She waved her lucky bear mascot.

'Just think about that glittering future!' shouted Elf, indiscreetly.

'Good luck!'

As the car moved away, Mrs Barry said:

'What glittering future's that, Rebecca?'

'Oh, only a joke,' said Rebecca quickly.

She couldn't tell Mrs Barry, not yet! It would be all round the staff room – Miss Welbeck would get to hear. And it wasn't even definite yet. And when the time came, it wouldn't be up to her to say anything. It would be up to her parents! They'd write a proper letter.

Her parents. They should have had her letter about a week ago – and one from Mr Lasky by now, surely? They weren't exactly rushing to reply. She'd been expecting to hear from them any day. No letter had arrived.

Perhaps they were up country, away from base. Or perhaps they needed time to reflect. Once they'd thought about it, they'd see what a wonderful opportunity it was for Rebecca, even though they weren't very interested in tennis themselves, wouldn't they?

Meanwhile, on the long car journey to her Great-Aunt Ivy's house in Bath, Rebecca had plenty of time herself to reflect. Leaning back palely against the headrest, palms partly clenched, her body taut and unrelaxed, she could feel the tension slowly building up inside her.

She'd burnt her boats now. She wasn't going to do as well in her GCSEs as she'd once hoped. Not even in the French. She wouldn't be going to Paris now. She'd have to tell M. Lafarge. She'd tell him next week. Emmanuelle would be upset. Perhaps M. Lafarge would be able to find someone else to go in her place.

She'd sacrificed everything: for the tennis.

So her whole future turned on the Bristol tournament now.

Mr Lasky would be there in person, watching her.

She mustn't lose a single match. She mustn't lose a single set. She mustn't lose a single game. She mustn't lose a single POINT!

The pressure was on.

TEN

BREAK POINT

'You're very irritable, young lady, if you don't mind my saying so,' said Great-Aunt Ivy on the Sunday night. 'Surely you can wash up those few dishes for me? Wait till you're old with arthritic hands like mine, that's all I can say! I don't mind cooking you a nice supper when you come in from your tennis, but I don't see why I should have to wash up the dishes as well.'

'Sorry, Aunty Ivy,' sighed Rebecca. She felt like screaming at her father's aunt. She did go on so! 'I only said I was going to do them in a minute.'

'You said it rather rudely, my girl. When I was fifteen years of age I didn't answer back . . .'

Rebecca went over to the sink and started washing up, trying to close her ears to the sound of the old lady's wearisome, plaintive tones. At the same time she felt rather ashamed of herself. She had been snappy just now about the dishes. Poor old Aunty, she lived on her own, she was used to her little routine. When Rebecca had stayed with her before, they'd got along all right. It only required a little kindness, being patient, listening to all Aunty's troubles and making a bit of a fuss of her.

But this weekend was different. Everything about this tournament was different.

Rebecca's nerves felt stretched taut, like worn-out elastic, stretched and stretched and about to snap at any minute.

It was the tournament that was doing it.

And tomorrow would be the big crunch.

She'd be playing Rachel Cathcart in the final. She'd always known they'd be rivals but of course she'd never dreamt they'd be playing for the same stakes.

Last year's four semi-finalists having moved up to become 18–U players, Rachel and Rebecca had been placed in the opposite halves of the draw. They were seeded to meet each other in the final.

Rebecca arrived at the tournament on the Saturday morning to discover that, because of her brilliant perform-ance in that senior inter-county fixture last weekend, she was top seed for the 16–U! She was expected to defeat Rachel, the number two seed, and win the tournament!

It was an awesome responsibility and did nothing to ease her tension.

Nor did Rachel's parents. Mr and Mrs Cathcart were very much in evidence. They'd booked into a hotel right next to the beflagged stadium and they stuck around like limpets. They complained about the seeding, saying that their daughter should have been the top seed. They com-plained loudly and bitterly about any close line calls that went against their daughter. They verbally abused their daughter after each match and told her everything she'd done wrong. They were, according to dressing-room gossip, a menace and had been banned from several junior tournaments last season.

The reason for their heightened tension at Bristol soon became obvious to Rebecca.

It was because Mr Lasky was there.

Rebecca spotted the bespectacled, middle-aged man in the bright blue jacket on the first morning, during her opening-round match. He was sitting next to Miss Brogan, in the best seats, right behind the canvas. Miss Brogan waved to her at one point as she was changing ends, so Rebecca knew that the man in the next seat must be the famous agent.

She won her first match comfortably, but by the time she came off court the couple had already left their seats.

However, Rachel Cathcart was on next, and the couple immediately reappeared. That was when Rebecca realized.

You can count on Mr Lasky coming to Bristol in person, Brenda Brogan had told her, the day she'd driven her back to school. *You'll be the second young player he'll be watching there.*

Of course! Rachel Cathcart.

She was that second young player. She, like Rebecca, was in with a chance of a contract.

If any further confirmation were needed, the looks that Mr and Mrs Cathcart gave Rebecca over the course of the weekend told her everything she needed to know.

The Cathcarts were ordinary people themselves, but from the moment they'd realized that Rachel's remarkable talent for tennis might one day make the family's fortune, everything else in their lives had taken second place.

Now this fair-haired girl called Rebecca Mason, this upstart who'd appeared from nowhere in the last couple of years, could possibly stand in the way of the contract for Rachel they'd worked so hard for!

If looks could kill, Rebecca would have died several times over, that weekend.

But all this remained unspoken. As for Herman Lasky and the glamorous Brenda Brogan, they kept their heads down. They never came near either player while the tournament was running its course. They were just silent figures on the sidelines, making notes, watching each girl's tennis (first round, second round, quarter finals, semi-finals) as Rebecca and Rachel progressed inexorably to Monday's final.

'You look pale, Rebecca,' said Mrs Barrington. 'Are you sure you feel all right?'

'I'm fine, Mrs Barry,' Rebecca replied edgily.

It was mid-morning on the Monday. Mrs Barrington had come to collect Rebecca from Great-Aunt Ivy's house. Rebecca's suitcase was in the hall, ready packed. They'd be going back to Trebizon this evening.

'We'll be popping back to Bath after the match, Rebecca,' her housemistress explained, as Rebecca gave her great-aunt a dry little peck on the cheek. 'You can collect your case then.' Mrs Barry smiled at the elderly lady. 'I'm sure Miss Mason will want to hear how you got on.'

Lady Bacon, the old schoolfriend with whom Mrs Barry had been staying in Bath, was sitting in the car. Joan Barrington was beginning to enjoy these annual trips, driving Rebecca to the Bristol tournament, then shopping and sightseeing in Bath with her oldest friend. She was delighted that Rebecca had reached the final this year, so she'd bought tickets for Georgina and herself. Rebecca's great-aunt hadn't wanted one.

She'd be giving her friend a lift back to Bath afterwards, and collecting her own case. So Rebecca could say her goodbyes to her relative then. Surely old Miss Mason would want to hear how her great-niece had done?

'We're looking forward to this, Rebecca,' said Mrs Barry as she drove out of the lovely Roman city and took the Bristol road. 'Aren't we, Georgina?'

'Yes, indeed,' said Lady Bacon. 'I've heard so much about you, Rebecca.'

Rebecca just sat there, stiff with tension. Why had Mrs Barry brought her friend to watch? Did she have to?

She'd never felt so lonely in her life.

She had no one to talk to. Twice, as Mrs Barry had driven her into Bristol, she'd almost blurted everything out – just how much was at stake this weekend. But each time her mouth had gone dry and she'd fallen silent.

Rachel Cathcart was insufferable.

Dark-haired, very pretty, very tough – and a showoff. She seemed to have an unlimited supply of stunning tennis outfits, and one of those white tennis jackets that Rebecca had always wanted.

In the dressing-rooms yesterday, just before Rebecca's semi-final, she'd said, demoralizingly:

'I think clothes are awfully important, don't you, Rebecca? To how one plays? Don't you find those tops a bit boring? You ought to get some sponsorships. Mummy and Daddy got me a contract with Dee Designs, aren't they clever?'

'I get my rackets free,' Rebecca had replied snappily. She had four altogether; she was testing the tension on one of them right now. Good. Just how she liked it. 'That's enough to be going on with.'

Brave words. She'd walked out on court five minutes

later, wondering if the entire crowd was staring critically at her boring tennis top.

Each day, too, masses of flowers arrived for Rachel. She seemed to have a lot of boyfriends.

Rebecca received one small bouquet. Carnations, with a small card tucked amongst them: *Good luck. Robbie. xxxx.* She was almost moved to tears by them, by the fact that Robbie had remembered and been thoughtful.

But they didn't look much beside all Rachel's flowers.

Rebecca knew that she was being rather silly. If only her friends had been around, to talk to! How they'd laugh at someone like Rachel Cathcart. What wouldn't Tish be saying! In fact, if Rebecca hadn't hated her so much, she'd have felt deeply sorry for the girl. Her parents were monsters! They were turning their daughter into one, too!

So it was that Rebecca felt completely alone.

She'd gone to bed early on Sunday night after the little wrangle over the washing-up, exhausted by the day's matches. This morning she'd breakfasted late. Now she was being driven to Bristol. She'd have a glucose drink when she got there, then half an hour's warm-up on one of the outside courts. Then . . .

At two o'clock; the final.

She'd chosen tennis, hadn't she? She'd let everything else slide, hadn't she? So she couldn't and she mustn't fail. Her inside felt like a tightly coiled spring.

At the competitors' entrance to the stadium, Rebecca handed Mrs Barrington something before they went their separate ways.

It was her battered old teddy bear, Biffy.

'Will you hold him for me during the match, Mrs Barry?' she pleaded.

'Of course I will, Rebecca.'
Both women thought how tense she looked.

Rebecca was barely conscious of the crowd; or of Rachel Cathcart's parents in the front row, leaning forward, noses over the canvas, almost falling into the court. She was conscious only of Mr Lasky, sitting there in his usual seat. And of her opponent, Rachel herself.

What a slippery customer she was. So tenacious. Her serve seemingly impossible to break.

Every point had to be fought for, with long and exhausting rallies. Every game had gone to deuce. Rebecca felt as though the match had been dragging on for hours, as though she'd already played several sets. But it was still only the first set!

Six games all in the first set.

'Tie-break,' announced the umpire.

Rebecca ground her teeth. She knew she had to win this tie-break. She knew she had to win this set. If she lost this set, she'd lose the match!

Rachel served first. An ace. 1–0.

Rebecca then served a fault. Her second serve was too short. Rachel put it away. 2–0. Rebecca's next serve was fast and an exciting rally followed, which she lost. 3–0 to Rachel.

Then her opponent became over-confident, putting two smashes out and returning Rebecca's next service into the net.

3–3. Change ends.

Rebecca towelled her face and hands, on the way. She could hear Mr Cathcart snarling something at his daughter. But there was only one thing Rebecca cared about.

Winning.

The next four points produced quite dazzling rallies,

each girl fighting as though her life depended on it. Rebecca levelled the score at 5–5 with a brilliant serve, followed up by a winning volley that brought applause from the crowd.

Rebecca took a deep breath.

She had one serve left, then it would be Rachel to serve again. And she was almost invincible on her service. So if Rebecca let Rachel break her service on this point, she'd almost certainly lose the tie-break; the set; and, most likely, the match.

Rebecca took two more deep breaths, to steady herself, the way Robbie had taught her. She must make it a perfect serve, an ace. She threw the ball up, straight, true, arched her back and swung the racket right back so that it touched between her shoulder blades as her coaches had shown her a hundred times . . .

A tremendous swing, a twist of the racket head, to get spin. Bring it down . . .

Contact!

An ace – surely an ace!

The service fizzed almost unstoppably. Rachel lunged. Got her racket to it. And hit it into the net.

'FAULT!'

Rebecca stared in disbelief. She felt as though she were breaking apart.

'No!' she screamed.

She ran over to the umpire's chair. Press cameras were flashing. She heard her own voice, as though from a long way off, as though it were someone else's voice:

'That call was crazy!' she shouted in a white rage. 'That serve was in! It wasn't out – it was in!'

The umpire was already saying something into his microphone:

'Over-rule. The serve was in. Miss Mason leads 6–5.'

Pandemonium broke out. Rachel threw her racket down.

'It was called out!' she cried. 'You've got to be joking! How could I hit it properly when it was called out!'

Rachel's father was on his feet, somewhere behind the umpire's chair, hurling abuse.

'The serve was out! Get your eyes tested!'

'Fool! Fool!' screamed his wife.

Two uniformed stewards started moving forward in their direction.

Dazed, trembling, Rebecca walked back to the baseline, waiting for play to resume. Rachel was up by the umpire's chair. 'How could I play it properly when it was called out!'

Two stewards were escorting Mr and Mrs Cathcart out of the stadium.

Herman Lasky and Brenda Brogan were exchanging delighted looks.

Mrs Barrington and her friend, Lady Bacon, were exchanging looks of dismay.

The crowd was starting a slow handclap, some youngsters calling out: 'Play a let! Why don't you play a let?'

The umpire remonstrated with Rachel and then took control of the microphone and the situation.

'Bad call. The ball was in. Miss Cathcart hit the ball *before* the bad call. Miss Mason leads by 6 points to 5. Play will now resume.'

Rachel took a while to settle down after that and it cost her dearly. For Rebecca won the next point and with it the tie-break 7–5, and the first set. She then broke Rachel's service immediately and went on to take the second set, 6–4, thereby winning the match, the tournament, and a replica silver rose-bowl.

She also won some praise from the great Mr Lasky in person, who shook her by the hand with unconcealed pleasure before he drove away with Miss Brogan. He'd decided that Rebecca Mason was probably very marketable.

'A great performance and I mean performance,' he told her. He'd very much enjoyed the instant ferocity between Mason and Cathcart. In his mind, it had never been a question of either/or. He was interested in offering both girls a contract. How they'd fight! What crowds they might pull in, one of these days! Even this little fracas was going to make the newspapers! But, of course, there had been no point in letting them know that. 'Produce a repeat perform-ance at Edgbaston and the contract's yours, Rebecca. I haven't heard back from your parents but I dare say I will.'

Noting Rebecca's strained look, he added:

'Don't worry about the Cathcart parents. They'll be written right out of any contract Rachel gets from me. Their behaviour was appalling.'

'And mine, too, Mr Lasky,' said Rebecca.

Mrs Barrington was looking for her so she said goodbye.

Disgusted with herself, Rebecca gave the rose-bowl to her great-aunt. 'It'll be lovely on the hall table, Aunty Ivy,' she said. 'You can fill it with all your best flowers this summer. You can tell all your friends I won it for you, at Bristol!'

The old lady dabbed at it in awe, with a lace handkerchief.

'It's beautiful, Rebecca. It's really beautiful. Oh, my dear, I'm so pleased to see you yourself again. You take this tennis much too seriously. You haven't been yourself this time!'

'I hope I haven't,' said Rebecca. She embraced her father's aunt and clung to her for a moment, for reassur-ance. 'I haven't liked myself this weekend. Not one bit. Especially not today.'

Winning the tournament was one thing.

Losing all respect for yourself in the process was something different again.

ELEVEN

AN AIRMAIL PACKET

'Your behaviour was dreadful, Rebecca,' said Mrs Barrington, when at last they were alone together in the car, heading westwards back to Trebizon.

The housemistress was furious with her charge. Furious that Rebecca had let her down in front of her oldest friend. Georgina's final words, back at the house, still rankled: *Old school's going downhill, isn't it? Hadn't you better get a grip on that girl, Joan?*

She was furious, too, that she'd had to struggle through a bevy of reporters with Rebecca, fending off their bombardment of questions with a volley of *No comments*! As though her Fifth Year pupil were some jumped-up little film star. But they'd taken photographs. This would be in the *Western Daily Press* tomorrow, and no mistake. 'Trebizon Girl Screams at Umpire.' Miss Welbeck would ask some awkward questions.

What on earth was happening to Rebecca Mason?

'It was quite dreadful,' she repeated.

'I know it was, Mrs Barry,' replied Rebecca, in a dull voice. 'You don't have to tell me.'

She half dozed in the front passenger seat, drained of all emotion, watching the bare trees that lined the roads rise up one by one towards her. She felt no sense of elation that she'd won the tournament, with the contract beginning to look a near certainty. She just felt tired, tired; overwhelmed by conflicting thoughts.

So Mr Lasky had been hoping to take *both* of them on, all along! He'd actually enjoyed seeing her lose her self-control like that, creating a scene, exciting the crowd! He'd enjoyed the way Rachel Cathcart had responded in kind. He liked their attitude – win at any price.

'You couldn't possibly have known whether your service was in or out, Rebecca,' stated Mrs Barry. 'You couldn't possibly see! You were at the far end of the court!'

That was something else Rebecca didn't need to be told.

Of course she couldn't see! It was just that she'd so badly *wanted* the serve to be in; as though her whole future, her whole life, had depended on it.

'The umpire's in a position to judge, not you, Rebecca! He'd already decided the ball was in. But it could just as easily have been out.'

Rebecca said nothing. They travelled on in silence, the car engine humming smoothly. Rebecca cradled Biffy on her lap. Even the one-armed bear seemed to be gazing up at her in silent reproach. Occasionally she fingered the little silver brooch that was pinned to her sweater: crossed tennis rackets, from Robbie last year. He'd be so thrilled that she'd won the tournament; so would Gran, who had written back as soon as she'd received Rebecca's letter. So would her friends.

Yes, they'll all be pleased, mused Rebecca, without emotion.

She was half dozing again when Mrs Barry said suddenly:

'Who were that man and woman I saw you talking to?'

Rebecca was startled. She hadn't realized she'd been seen!

'Just – just –'

'Who, Rebecca?'

So Rebecca told her.

Mrs Barry was frowning. She seemed to be concentrating on picking up the road-signs in the car's headlights. They'd be joining the motorway in a minute. After she'd successfully manoeuvred the car round a roundabout, down a slip-road and into the stream of motorway traffic, she spoke again.

'So this man, Mr Lasky, he's an agent? Is he interested in you?'

'Yes.'

'I see. How interested?'

They were driving due west, the car purring now, the night sky ahead of them touched with the last embers of the sunset, terracotta and gold. They were coming over a hill and a ribbon of red tail-lights snaked across the plain below, the white headlights of oncoming cars mere pinpricks of light.

'How interested, Rebecca?'

Rebecca blurted it all out. It was a relief to do so.

Mrs Barry went very quiet. At last, sounding disturbed, she said:

'So we might be losing you this summer, Rebecca?'

'Well. Yes. I suppose so.'

'The glittering future?' she added, and Rebecca felt discomforted. 'You should have confided in me. I wondered what was wrong with you. You've been rather strange lately. No wonder you've let your school work slide! It must all seem very exciting, very attractive. Lots of money. Lots of clothes. Lots of tennis. Fame! And you're sure that's what you want, Rebecca?'

She didn't answer.

'And what about your parents?' her housemistress asked finally. 'Do they know about this? How do they feel about it?'

'I'm waiting to hear from them,' said Rebecca. 'They should have written by now.'

Mrs Barry turned on the car radio; there was a concert she wanted to listen to.

'Perhaps there'll be something waiting for you when we get back to the house,' she said, bringing the conversation to an end.

And there was.

It was an airmail packet from Saudi Arabia, much thicker than an ordinary letter. Rebecca wondered what her parents could possibly be sending her.

When she'd got back to Trebizon, quite late, Court House was in darkness apart from the Barringtons' private wing, for of course school was still on half-term. Mr Barrington had appeared as soon as the car had been parked, offering Rebecca supper. But she didn't feel even slightly hungry.

'I think I'd rather just go up and have a bath and an early night,' she'd said. 'Thanks all the same.'

'There's some post for you, Rebecca,' he'd said then, and found the packet for her.

Rebecca took it, went through to the main building, thanked Annie, the assistant matron, for putting on the lights for her, then hurried up the three flights of stairs to her floor. The packet was now in her weekend luggage.

It was an hour before she opened it.

Just as she'd had to prepare herself mentally to write to

her parents, she now found it necessary to go through the same process before reading their reply.

She unpacked. Had a bath. Got changed into her pyjamas. Went along to the little kitchen and made herself a cup of cocoa. Finally, entering the warmth and privacy of her cubicle, she switched on the bedside light and climbed into bed.

She took a few sips of cocoa and only then, cocooned in her duvet, fingers trembling slightly, did she open the packet.

The letter from her parents was not very long. She quickly read it through.

Then she flicked it over. Clipped behind the letter were two thickish documents, each with the Trebizon school crest on the front.

Her last two school reports! The one her parents had received at Christmas and the one they'd received last summer, at the end of the Fourth Year. The Christmas one had been posted to them abroad. The Fourth Year one had been handed to them personally by Miss Welbeck, when they'd visited her at the end of the summer term. Rebecca knew that Miss Welbeck had discussed it with them at the time and that afterwards they'd been unusually secretive, refusing to let her know what was in it. She turned to that one first.

She skimmed through the various teachers' comments, the record of her marks in the summer exams; finally reaching the principal's summing-up, written in Miss Welbeck's beautifully formed, scholarly handwriting:

Rebecca has inevitably failed to reach her true potential in some of her academic subjects owing to the demands that her outstanding talent for tennis has placed upon her.

Nevertheless, she is emerging as a most gifted linguist and her essay writing is of the highest order. She is clearly a candidate for a top university and in time will have difficult choices to make which cannot be imposed on her but must be hers alone.

Madeleine Welbeck

On the more recent report, written at Christmas, Miss Welbeck's summing-up was much briefer:

Due to her injury, Rebecca has been able to give wholehearted attention to her school work this term and has made remarkable progress. This confirms the observations that I made last summer and the fact that difficult choices lie ahead.

Madeleine Welbeck

Rebecca had to read all this through two or three times before it would sink in properly. Gifted? Top university?

She then turned back to her parents' letter, which began:

Dear Rebecca,
Thank you for your letter! We've thought long and hard about your exciting news. We've also heard from Mr Lasky. He sounds very nice. Your mother and I wouldn't want to stand in the way of such a wonderful opportunity if this is really what you want to do, though we're worried that you're rather young to have to make such an important decision.

We didn't want to show you your school report last summer, because we've never wanted to put any pressure on you. But we feel you ought to see it now, so that you can consider all the options. We're also sending the one we received at Christmas, and have written to Miss Welbeck to explain our reason for doing this . . .

Rebecca read through this part of the letter, the important part, several times and then finally put everything away in her locker.

By then her cocoa was cold, but she drank it just the same. She tried to think about things but by now her brain felt as numb as her emotions had been, ever since that uncontrollable outburst on court. This airmail packet only made things worse. She wanted to sleep! To sleep and sleep . . . and sleep.

She woke late on the Tuesday morning. The first thing that struck her was the eerie silence. Where was everybody? Where were her friends?

It was lovely to be back at Trebizon, but where were they?

She sat up in bed. She could see particles of dust rising from her duvet in the shaft of early spring sunshine that fell from the skylight.

'Tish? Sue?' she called sleepily.

Then she remembered. They were all away on half-term, but they'd be coming back this afternoon. And Cliff was coming over, coming to lunch!

Then she remembered everything else.

It engulfed her, like a black cloud. She suddenly felt miserable, filled with regrets. Why? Why?

She was almost certain of the contract now, wasn't she? She'd be able to play tennis all the time! She'd have lovely clothes to wear. She'd travel to lots of exciting places and she'd work and work to be the best – hadn't she always secretly wanted that, to be the best? Fame!

Mr Lasky liked her.

Only she didn't like Mr Lasky that much. And she didn't like herself either – not that other self, the one on court yesterday, the one that Mr Lasky had liked.

Her eyes strayed to her work-table; to the piles of school work stacked there. Half-finished essays. Books to revise for mocks that she hadn't even started. Mocks started this Friday! She hadn't a hope! She'd chosen tennis . . .

With a sudden aching sense of loss, Rebecca thought of all the friendships she'd be leaving behind.

Fifth Year friendships.

Tish and Sue and Margot and Elf and Mara. It would be unbearable to think of them all still here, doing things without her. And although Robbie wouldn't be around much longer, there was still Cliff. It was fun to have met up with Cliff again! And there were her three favourite teachers. Miss Heath, who'd taught her English all the way up the school. And dear old Maggy, such a brilliant history teacher – she loved it. She lived it. There was Pargie, too; especially him.

And Emmanuelle! They'd written such great letters to each other: Rebecca had been longing to meet her! There was the Dread, too. She'd even miss her. What would the Dread think of the way she'd behaved at Bristol?

Propped up in bed against the pillows, Rebecca closed her eyes and swallowed hard. In the silence she could hear the twittering and scampering of birds in the eaves above her dormer window. Were they starting to build a nest up there?

Gradually the awful truth sank in.

She didn't want to leave Trebizon! She didn't want to play at Edgbaston. She wanted to go to Paris at Easter! With all her friends. She wanted to see Emmanuelle. But it was too late. She hadn't sent the form back for Gran to sign!

She wanted to stay on at Trebizon and go into the Sixth and be editor of the *Trebizon Journal* and go to one of those top universities . . .

But she couldn't. She'd thrown it all away. She'd never get those good GCSE grades now . . .

'Rebecca!'

Mrs Barrington was standing beside her with a cup of tea.

'So you're awake at last,' she said gently. She smiled. 'Here, drink some tea and then get up. It'll have to be just muesli this morning. Put something respectable on. Miss Welbeck wants to see you at her house at half past ten.'

TWELVE

BACK TO NAOMI

Rebecca sat in Miss Welbeck's drawing-room, nervously nibbling at a chocolate biscuit. A copy of the morning's *Western Daily Press* lay open on the coffee table. It was upside down but she could see her photo and almost read the headline in quite largish type.

TEEN TANTRUMS – WAS THIS A FAIR WIN?

She averted her eyes from it; she didn't want to know what it said.

'I gather from your parents that you've been hoping to gain a professional tennis contract, Rebecca,' the principal had said calmly. 'But I now gather from Mrs Barrington that you may be having second thoughts?'

'Yes!' Rebecca had exclaimed in surprise. How had Mrs Barry guessed the truth, even before she'd realized it herself? 'I don't want the contract!' she'd added passionately. 'I want to stay at Trebizon!'

Miss Welbeck, having offered Rebecca a biscuit, had been about to pour out coffee. She'd suddenly replaced the coffee pot on the table, risen to her feet and walked over to the french windows.

She stood rooted in that position, her back firmly turned on Rebecca, apparently gazing at a bird perched on the sundial in the middle of her back lawn.

'You're sure about that?' she asked now, without a trace of emotion in her voice.

'Quite sure, Miss Welbeck.'

'And you've reached this decision entirely on your own, Rebecca? There's been no undue influence from any quarter?'

'None.'

Only then did the principal turn round. She no longer had to hide the radiant expression of relief on her face. She'd known Rebecca would have this painful choice to make quite soon, but not as soon as this! How had the Lasky man spotted her so quickly?

She came and sat opposite Rebecca and poured the coffee into delicate gold leaf cups and offered the sugar bowl and a jug of cream. She moved the newspaper off the table.

'I think we'd better just forget about this, Rebecca.'

'I'm so ashamed of it!' said Rebecca. 'I don't think I'll ever like myself on a tennis court again.'

'Nonsense!' said the principal. 'You'll always want to win but you'll never be under quite the same pressure again. When you go back into serious tennis, perhaps in a couple of years' time, you'll be in a different situation.'

'How's that?' asked Rebecca, in wonder.

'It will no longer be "all or nothing". You'll have achieved the excellent A level grades of which you're capable. You'll know that a place is waiting for you at university, to be taken up either then or later. Your options will have widened. You'll have the security of knowing that other interesting careers are open to you, should the tennis not work out for any reason.'

Cliff's words suddenly flashed into Rebecca's mind. *It's all right, unless you have another car accident, Rebecca!* Who'd ever have thought that Cliff could say something so sensible?

'But will I even get into the Sixth Form now?' Rebecca asked unhappily. 'I mean, don't you have to have good GCSEs?'

'There's still time, Rebecca,' said the principal. She rose to her feet, glancing at her watch. Miss Morgan was coming to see her shortly, about poor little Naomi Cook. 'Now that your mind's made up, I'll speak to Miss Willis on your behalf. I'm afraid I'll have to show her this newspaper report. She'll talk to Miss Darling about this and also to your county coach. It's quite essential that you have a complete break from tennis for the next few months. Your parents will write to Mr Lasky – and so shall I.' She smiled. 'Trebizon's going to be unpopular with the Lawn Tennis Association! First Josselyn Vining, now you. But *your* absence from the scene will be only temporary, I hope. I do understand how they feel,' she sighed. 'It's so long since we've won a Wimbledon singles title.'

'It's always been my favourite day-dream. Winning Wimbledon!' Rebecca said.

'Why not?' replied the principal. 'Virginia Wade did.'

'What do you mean exactly, Miss Welbeck?'

'Virginia had a maths degree from Sussex University but she still won Wimbledon.'

Rebecca was so preoccupied with this remark that it was

only at Miss Welbeck's front door that she remembered about Paris.

'I didn't send the form back for my grandmother to sign! I thought I'd be playing at Edgbaston.'

'Then you'd better go and post it now,' replied Miss Welbeck. 'I dare say M. Lafarge can cope with one late form, and book your travel tickets just the same.'

For the first time in weeks, Rebecca's *joie de vivre* returned.

Joy was also very much in evidence on the top floor of Court House that evening. Elf had brought a superb Dundee cake back from Scotland and they shared it with most of the floor.

'Rebecca might have been leaving!'

'Somebody was going to offer her a tennis contract!'

'But she doesn't want it. She's going to stay at Trebizon!'

Mara actually wept.

Robbie phoned through, aghast. It was too urgent for a letter this time.

'Rebeck, what's all this stuff I read in the paper?'

So she told him; everything.

'I bet he was shattered,' commented Sue, coming and sitting on the end of Rebecca's bed, just before Lights Out. 'Justy says he's been boasting about you around Garth and being mysterious for weeks.'

'Big fool!' grinned Tish, coming into the cubicle.

'He sounds as though he's going to get over it,' smiled Rebecca, propped up in bed, hands behind her head, staring at the ceiling. 'Anyway, he liked the birthday card I sent him.'

She was actually thinking about something else.

'Sue,' she said suddenly. 'You're doing Religious Studies

for GCSE, aren't you? There's a famous quotation from the Old Testament that I'm trying to remember.'

'Which book?'

Rebecca told her and Sue reeled it off.

'Yes, that's the one!' exclaimed Rebecca.

Tish said: 'What's all that about, Rebeck?'

'Nothing!'

But in fact a ridiculous thought that had first entered her head before tea-time, when Cliff had mentioned a name, began to take root. There would be no shaking it off.

Very soon now she must keep her promise to Holly Thomas, keep faith with Naomi Cook, and put that thought to the test.

Her own troubles receding, her mind had gone back to Naomi.

Cliff had, as usual, been effervescent company that day.

Even when, after a good lunch with the Barringtons and a run along the beach together, she'd dragged him into the common room with her maths books and forced him to give her some help!

'You've got to be joking, Rebecca. We're supposed to be on half-term. Why don't we just put these books away and watch the football?'

'We can't! The remote control's vanished!' laughed Rebecca, who'd just hidden it under a cushion. 'Come on, Cliff, you're the one who warned me off the tennis. We've just had a ceremonial burning on the beach of my Edgbaston entry form, haven't we? Please, Cliff! Mocks start on Friday and the first one's *maths*. It's no worse than watching football.'

When it was time for him to leave, just before tea-time,

she'd walked with him as far as main school. He'd wheeled his cycle alongside.

'I'll show you the short cut. There's another gate down on to the beach, from the copse behind Juniper House. It'll save you about half a mile.'

Rebecca was also keeping an eager look-out for her friends. The first coach from the station had just trundled past them and quite a few taxis as well.

As they crossed the cobbled yard at the back of Juniper House, they saw a taxi pull up. A short figure in a woollen dress got out with a small suitcase and paid the driver. It was Naomi Cook, back from the half-term holiday with her family, and not looking any the happier for it, Rebecca noted. Presumably that rusted old van of her father's had finally packed up as expected.

Deeply preoccupied, intent on reaching the junior boarding house, Naomi passed within a few metres of them, head down.

Cliff, who'd been in the middle of telling Rebecca a joke, suddenly turned his head and called:

'Hello, Ruthie. Want a lift?'

Startled, Naomi glanced round, stared straight through Cliff without recognition, then hurried on her way. She hadn't even noticed Rebecca.

'Cut it out, Cliff!' said Rebecca. Cliff acting stupid, as usual! 'Go away! I'm not with you – I don't think I know you!'

'I thought it was a kid at our school!' Cliff said, pretending to look hurt. 'Now, where was I –?'

He finished the joke and it made Rebecca laugh, a lot.

It was only after he'd gone that the unlikely thought entered her head, only to be dismissed as she raced back to Court House to see if her friends had arrived.

THIRTEEN

ACTION COMMITTEE TRIUMPH

It was Saturday afternoon. 'The six' were aching from head to foot. Holly Thomas was with them and she was aching, too. As a special privilege today, they'd let her join in the activities of the Senior Action Committee.

Or, rather, inactivities. They'd been hiding uncomfortably in the thick shrubbery at the back of Juniper House for well over an hour now!

From this hiding-place they had a perfect view over the cobbled courtyard behind the junior boarding house, across to the back door.

If the thief were someone from outside school, this would be their most likely point of entry. It would be so easy for them to come up from the beach, through the little wicket gate and then the copse. They'd hardly be likely to use Juniper's main entrance: the big double doors which fronted on to the school quadrangle. They'd be too easily seen.

The oak table in the hall, where Holly's Walkman had been left and, later, the chocolates, was visible from either entrance.

'*If* it's an outside person,' Holly had said dubiously, and Rebecca had glared at her.

Now, on a low wall by the back door, the bait had been temptingly placed.

'What shall we club together and buy then?' Tish had asked that morning. 'We can't do chocolates again, that's corny.'

'I'm not sure we need to buy anything, after all,' Rebecca had replied. She'd been giving the matter careful thought. 'I think your Gold would do very nicely, Tish.'

'WHA–AT? I don't want that pinched!'

The 'Gold', as it was called, was the brilliant red and gold striped scarf, with gold tassels, that only members of the school's First Hockey Eleven were allowed to own.

'We're going to be keeping watch, aren't we, Tish?' Mara had said, her brown eyes shining with excitement. She'd seen Rebecca in this sort of mood before. Mara, more than the others, sensed intuitively that Rebecca had some kind of secret theory of her own. Perhaps she already knew who the thief was!

She even seemed to know what time the thief usually came: not very long after lunch on a Saturday afternoon. Why else had she kept insisting that this was the best time to keep watch?

So here they were.

And there, on the little wall by the back door, was the gold-tasselled scarf.

But the sense of excitement that Rebecca had engendered was beginning to wear thin, even with Mara.

They'd been here since a quarter to two and it had now just turned three o'clock! At regular intervals juniors had passed in and out of the rear door, going about their business, walking straight by the scarf. As for an outside person, the only outside person who'd come by was the dairyman with ten huge crates of milk for the weekend.

'I'm stiff,' complained Elf.

'I'm fed up with having to crouch down all the time!' agreed Margot.

'My bad leg's hurting,' said Holly. She was very slightly lame. 'I don't think the thief's an outside person! If it's someone who's inside Juniper already they won't even see Tish's Gold! They could be indoors pinching something else right now.'

'Do shut up, Holly,' said Rebecca edgily.

'Oh, Rebecca,' said Mara anxiously, 'what about our maths?'

The first GCSE mock exam the previous day hadn't gone particularly well for either Rebecca or Mara. And another maths paper loomed on Monday.

Being reminded of exams completely unsettled everybody, even Tish.

'Oh, blow this for a bit of fun,' she said. 'We've all got plenty to do, especially you, Rebeck! Why don't we just pick up the Gold and go?'

'The junior action committee'll just have to work a bit harder, Holly,' said Elf apologetically. 'You'll have to go it alone.'

Rebecca felt a crushing sense of disappointment.

It looked as though her outlandish theory was just exactly that. Bizarre! She'd been leaping to conclusions, hadn't she, on very little evidence? Thank goodness she'd resisted the temptation to tell the others. Her own common sense had told her how silly the theory was . . .

'OK?' said Tish. She stood up from her hiding-place, her head showing over the top of the bushes; yawned and stretched. 'I'll just go and collect the Gold, shall I, and we'll call it a day – Hey?'

Rebecca had suddenly seized her by the arm and was dragging her back out of sight.

'Get down, Tish!' she hissed. 'Quickly! I heard something!'

A clanking sound, in the copse. There was someone there with a large bicycle, leaning it against a tree.

The small figure then came up through the copse from the direction of the beach, darting from tree to tree, furtively.

They all ducked and froze like statues as, a minute later, the girl appeared in the cobbled courtyard in front of them and tiptoed to the back door.

She glanced around, saw the scarf and started to finger it.

She looked around once more, to see if the coast was clear, then started to roll it up into a neat, tight bundle.

'Naomi Cook!' whispered Holly, breathless with excitement. 'May Ling was right all along!'

'And you were wrong, Rebeck,' whispered Sue, amazed.

Tish, seeing her precious scarf disappear, rolled up, inside the girl's denim jacket, yelled out:

'CHARGE!'

The other six surged out of the bushes, ran across the courtyard and grabbed her. She wriggled and squirmed and threshed around, but she couldn't escape.

'Got you, Naomi!'

'Hand over that scarf, please, it's the only one I've got.'

'You rotten little thief, Naomi! Where's my Walkman?'

Rebecca brought up the rear, taking her time.

'Let's have a look at her,' she said. 'Stand back a bit, can't you, Holly?'

The girl stopped struggling as Rebecca confronted her and gazed into her face. Yes, all the familiar features: small and pale, framed by fairish hair. Tearful.

But the expression was different. Sullen; rebellious.

'You're not Naomi, are you?' said Rebecca, indignantly. 'You're her twin sister, Ruth.'

'What of it!' cried the girl, and she burst into tears.

The rest of the Action Committee watched open-mouthed as Rebecca took the girl firmly by the arm and led her into the building, through to Miss Morgan's office.

Ten minutes later Miss Morgan's car left, with Ruth Cook inside and Mr Cook's old bicycle tied to the car's roof-rack. The junior housemistress drove to a big housing estate on the far fringes of the town, recovered Holly Thomas's Walkman, Jay Larcombe's blazer and an un-opened box of chocolates from their hiding-place in Ruth Cook's bedroom, and then returned to school.

Naomi meanwhile was still at netball practice.

When Cliff had called Naomi 'Ruthie', it struck a chord. The names Ruth and Naomi had started running through Rebecca's mind. Weren't they in the Bible? Weren't they famous for being completely inseparable? That same evening, quoting from the book of Ruth, Sue had confirmed her recollection.

The Ruth and Naomi in the Bible hadn't been twins, of course, but daughter-in-law and mother-in-law. But they'd been inseparable! If Mr and Mrs Cook had had twin baby girls, wouldn't those names have been rather appropriate? Or was she just letting her imagination run away with her . . . ?

She'd rung Cliff, on the Wednesday night, asking him

casually if he knew Ruthie's surname. She wasn't going to suggest that the girl might be a thief, it was such a crazy thought, really!

'Her surname? Haven't a clue!' Cliff had replied. 'She's just a kid I've teased once or twice at school for looking such a misery boots. Nothing *like* that other girl, really. I don't know why I thought it was her! What would she be doing visiting Holloway Prison, anyway?'

'Oh, Cliff!' Rebecca had smiled.

That should have been the end of it.

After all, it was just too fantastic to imagine that Naomi had a twin sister and had kept it secret. That would be ludicrous. If you had a twin you'd be bound to talk about her at school.

Yet the thought persisted. Partly because of the girl she'd caught the merest glimpse of, cycling up the lane that day. And partly because of the two words Cliff had used: 'misery boots'.

A picture had flashed into her mind. Of a sullen face pressed to the rear window of that rusted van, somewhere off the motorway, when she'd been coming back to school at the beginning of term.

Such an uncharacteristic expression, she hadn't even been sure that it *was* Naomi.

Well, supposing it *hadn't* been? Supposing she did have a twin, called Ruth, and that had been Ruth's face at the window, refusing to get out of the van, refusing even to come out to the coach and see Naomi off?

All this simmered in the back of Rebecca's mind as she pored over her books, preparing for her mock GCSEs, bracing herself for the first exam on Friday.

And it wasn't till Saturday morning that it hit her – what May Ling had said in Moffatt's!

'I thought it was Naomi, it looked like her. But the face, well maybe . . . maybe it wasn't Naomi's expression.'

How crushing Rebecca had been! But was it possible? Had the little Chinese girl hit the nail right on the head?

There was no more time to be lost!

Rebecca had insisted that the Action Committee (senior version) be revivified! She'd dragged them – reluctant except for Mara, and of course young Holly, murmuring about their mocks – back into battle.

And they'd triumphed again!

FOURTEEN

FIFTH YEAR FRIENDSHIPS

'What an amazing story!' sighed Mara, on the Sunday afternoon.

Tempted by the watery sunshine, 'the six' were sitting out on the balcony, spilling down the fire escape, too, taking a break from their books. It was spring that had brought them outside. Spring was arriving! The snowdrops had gone, the crocuses were dying back and the first flowering of daffodils had begun, splashes of yellow in the Court House garden down below.

'Amazing,' agreed Margot. She sat at the top of the metal staircase, her long black legs drawn up, chin resting on knees. 'It's like something out of a book.'

'The Book of Ruth,' said Sue.

'What was that quotation, Sue?' asked Tish. 'Give it to us again.'

'Ruth, Chapter One,' said Sue. 'Ruth pleads with Naomi:

'"Intreat me not to leave thee, or to return from following after thee: for whither thou goest, I will go; and where thou lodgest, I will lodge: thy people shall be my people, and thy

God my God: Where thou diest, will I die, and there will I be buried."'

They all fell silent.

'What I can't understand, Rebeck,' said Tish, after a while, 'is why the School Governors didn't offer to split the top scholarship between them, seeing they scored identical marks.'

'But they did!' explained Rebecca. She'd had a long, long talk with Naomi the night before. 'And put some more money towards it as well, as much as the bursary fund would stand, to make it a two-thirds scholarship each. But that meant Mr and Mrs Cook would still have to find something. It was impossible for them. The twins thought it was silly that *one* of them shouldn't benefit and have the free place so –' Rebecca swallowed hard. 'They tossed a coin. Would you believe it? A coin. And Naomi won.'

'But that's terrible!' said Tish, in horror.

Rebecca nodded.

'Yes. They thought it was a brilliant idea at the time but it was stupid. They'd no idea how much they were going to miss each other. On top of that, Ruth's school was terrible and she got bullied, and she got more and more resentful that Naomi had been the 'lucky' one. And Naomi got more and more miserable because she felt so guilty that she'd won the toss. Miss Morgan kept trying to get her to talk about her twin, but she'd start crying every time the name Ruth was mentioned, so Miss Morgan gave up. It was a no-go area.'

Rebecca continued: 'Well, anyway, the family moved down here after Christmas, they were so worried. They knew Caxton High was a good school, because they've got some relatives here, on the same estate. And they thought the twins would feel better, knowing they weren't so far apart.'

'But it just made things worse?' hazarded the others.

'Yes. So near and yet so far! That was the effect it had on Naomi. And of course poor little Ruth, catching glimpses of Trebizon uniform around the town, well – it just constantly reminded her! Made her feel even more furious. Also, they'd made these secret plans to meet in Juniper's copse on Saturday afternoons, the only time Ruth's dad doesn't miss his bike because he's always glued to *Grandstand*! And *that* soon turned sour –'

'Because Naomi got roped in for netball practice?' exclaimed Elf. 'Why didn't she make up an excuse to Jay?'

'Because she's too honest,' said Rebecca.

They all looked at her.

'You always said she was honest,' admitted Sue.

'I think I must have seen Ruth once!' Margot suddenly realized. 'Going into Woolworths. I thought it was Naomi. I thought she must have got permission.'

Rebecca gazed into space. She reflected that Ruth must actually have been carrying the Walkman, that day she saw her from the car, with Robbie. In the big toolbox on the back of her father's bike!

'So then Ruth started coming anyway,' said Tish. 'D'you think she planned to pinch things?'

'I'm sure she didn't,' said Rebecca. 'I think she just hoped each time that Naomi might cut netball practice and stick to the original plan. Then this compulsion would come over her: the need to compensate, for not getting her fair share! After all, she'd won the scholarship, too – so why shouldn't she take something of Trebizon back home with her!'

Later, Rebecca discovered that once or twice, secretly in her bedroom at nights, Ruth had dressed herself in Jay Larcombe's blazer, plugged Holly's earphones in and listened to the Walkman, the unopened box of chocolates beside her. Pretending she was at Trebizon! Pretending that she and Naomi were there together, having fun, and this was their dormitory.

'I've got to go now,' said Rebecca, looking at her watch. She got to her feet. She'd promised to help Naomi pack her trunk. 'See you at the tea party then? Four o'clock. Don't be late, or I'll kill you.'

'What d'you think we are?' protested Sue.

In spite of all that had passed, the little leaving party that Miss Morgan gave for Naomi, in her own flat, was not an unhappy occasion. She'd rustled up some delicious eats from the school cooks: little flaky sausage rolls, cheese-flavoured crisps, platefuls of iced fairy cakes and a huge chocolate sponge with cream in the middle.

Naomi was dignified and composed, at peace with herself at last. How much better she looks now! thought Rebecca.

The 'six' had been invited, Tish's Action Committee, as well as its junior version – Holly, Harriet, Sara and May. And Jay Larcombe. And two girls from One Alpha that Naomi particularly liked and had wanted to be there.

'I was going to put you in the netball team next week, Naomi,' Jay said regretfully. 'You'll make Caxton High's junior team, I'm sure.'

'When you come and play us, we won't know who to cheer for,' May Ling added sweetly.

Holly Thomas, discomforted by the whole situation, had agonized with Sue about making a present of her new Walkman to the twins! 'Their parents would never let them accept it,' Sue had pointed out.

But earlier, while they were packing the trunk, Rebecca had given Naomi a leaving present, two of her tennis rackets.

'Are you sure?' asked Naomi, gazing at them in delight.

'Of course I'm sure!' Rebecca had exclaimed. 'I get them free!' *At least I did*, she thought – remembering. She smiled. 'You and Ruth should try it. It's not a bad game. And you'll like Caxton High,' she added. She knew it was a good school; as good as Trebizon though very different. 'My friend Cliff will keep a look-out for you. I'll get news of you through Cliff.'

'Does that mean we can still be, well, sort of friends, Rebecca?' Naomi had asked then.

'Always!' nodded Rebecca.

After the party, Rebecca waited behind to help load Naomi's things into Miss Morgan's car. It was time to see her off.

As they stood by the car, there came the sound of footsteps across the cobbles. Rebecca turned and saw Miss Welbeck. The principal had walked all the way over from her house to say goodbye in person.

As juniors crowded at the windows to watch, Miss Welbeck took Naomi's hand. Rebecca thought how elegant she looked, in a beautiful designer suit; the wavy hair, touched with grey, framing the scholarly face.

'Goodbye, Naomi. Our loss will be your new school's gain. You are going to do very, very well, you know. I expect great things of you. I expect to hear your name spoken in years to come.'

As the car drove away, Rebecca and Miss Welbeck watched in silence.

Rebecca was overcome with emotion. How superficial her problems had been this term, compared with Naomi Cook's. How pleased she was to be staying at Trebizon! How lucky that Dad's firm paid her fees! The courage of the diminutive First Year girl in the situation in which she'd found herself was really quite humbling. She *would* keep in touch. She and Cliff, they'd try to be like a big brother and sister to the Cook twins.

So many Fifth Year friendships to be grateful for! thought Rebecca. Pargie and Maggy and Miss Heath. She'd try not to disappoint them. And Robbie and Cliff. And Tish and Sue and Margot and Elf – and Mara! And Emmanuelle! It was only a few weeks now before she'd be going to Paris.

And Naomi Cook.

'Yes, I expect great things of her,' murmured Miss Welbeck, standing next to Rebecca, shoulder to shoulder.

She turned and their eyes met for a moment.

'And of you, too, Rebecca.'

The principal smiled then and consulted her watch. She raised an eyebrow.

'Off you go then, Rebecca. Haven't you got exams tomorrow?'

ALLY, ALLY, ASTER
Ann Halam

Richard and Laura aren't very keen on making friends with the next door neighbour's pale, cold daughter, Ally, when they move to the isolated cottages on Cauldhouse Moor. There's something strange, almost inhuman, about her. But it's only as the bitter winter winds and snow draw in around the bleak moors that Richard and Laura discover that Ally is more than a little icy . . .

SUMMER OF A LIFETIME
Brigid Chard

Dan feels a failure – and when he is sent to his uncle's farm to recover from an operation, his confidence is at its lowest ebb. But soon not getting into his brothers' school ceases to seem so important as Dan's priorities change and his life finds a new direction. Who could have guessed at the thrill of snaring a rabbit, seeing a calf born, or training your very own ferret? Under the expert guidance of wily old ex-gamekeeper Ben Hugget, Dan develops skills he never dreamt he had and gradually learns a new self-respect.

THE MINERVA PROGRAM
Claire Mackay

Here at last is Minerva's chance to be out in front, to be really good at something – computers. That's where her future lies. But that future is threatened when Minerva is almost too clever for her own good. Suddenly she is accused of cheating and is banned from the computer room. It takes the combined talents of 'Spiderman', her brother, and her inventive friends to solve this intriguing mystery.

ROSCOE'S LEAP
Gillian Cross

To Hannah, living in a weird and fantastical old house means endlessly having to fix things like heating systems and furnaces, but for Stephen it is a place where something once happened to him, something dark and terrifying which he doesn't want to remember but cannot quite forget. Then a stranger intrudes upon the family and asks questions about the past that force Hannah to turn her attention from mechanical things to human feelings, and drive Stephen to meet the terror that is locked away inside him, waiting . . .

OVER THE MOON AND FAR AWAY
Margaret Nash

The new girl at school calls herself a 'traveller' and says she comes from beyond the stars. Ben doesn't believe her, of course, but then again Zillah isn't quite like anyone he and his friends have ever met. There's her name for a start, and she doesn't know how to play their games. But the mysterious new-comer does seem able to make things happen . . .

THE TROUBLE WITH JACOB
Eloise McGraw

Right from the start there is something very weird about the boy Andy sees on the hillside. Every time Andy's twin sister Kat is there he just disappears, and all he ever talks about is his bed! Andy thinks he's going mad, but then he and Kat decide that someone is playing tricks on them. There must be some logical solution to the mystery. After all, the only other explanation would be far too incredible . . .